Other books by Ron Frazer

Novels:

    Beyond a Veil

    Millennium 3

    The Carib's Smile

    The Judge's Wife

    The Wife's Turn

    A Handful of Seawater

Nonfiction:

    Staying Well: a family guide to wellness

    Healthier Happier Now

    Choosing to Heal

Websites:

    https://ronfrazer.com

    https://ronfrazer.com/blog

    https://facebook.com/RonFrazerAuthor

Time Branches

Maryam Press

Time Branches

by Ron Frazer

Third Edition

Buy additional copies of the book at:

https://ronfrazer.com

or your favorite bookseller

for Maryam

Acknowledgments

My friends Donna Amend, Ken Sloan, David Thomas, Bob Bartz, and my wife, Sandy Frazer, have been so kind and helpful with comments and suggestions while reading the earlier drafts.

Chapter 1

CAILYN TO MYSELF: *This is weird, really weird.*

CAILYN TO YOU: I'm dying from cancer. Well, that might not be true; I'm also in a coma. Stupid fall—one second at the top of the stairs, the next at the bottom, in a pile. I don't really remember any of it.

My first memory is hovering around inside an ambulance, looking down on two medics rapidly working on my body which was strapped to a spine board. Later, in the ER of a Cleveland hospital, excited people were scurrying around my body for a long time, poking, prodding and x-raying. Once things calmed down a bit, other people put the body here, in intensive care. I could say, "... put me here," but it doesn't seem like me down there.

Looking down on that dying body reminds me of the times when I was about to walk out of a bad movie, but stood at the door looking back at the screen for a few lines of dialogue because I thought I shouldn't waste the price of admission. So I look down on that carcass and think, *What a waste!* All the years of primping, exercising, dieting and what did it get me? The worrying over a job, or a boyfriend, or an income tax form—it all falls into place, a fairly meaningless place, at that.

It's 2018, probably September. My mother, Lottie

Whittaker, seventy-five years old, is sitting by the bed, holding the body's right hand, the one without any tubes attached, staring blankly across the body at the hardware that is keeping her fifty-five-year-old daughter alive. Mom looks numb. She's been here for days, looking worse each day.

> *Look at her! I wish I could move a finger to let her know it's OK. Hell, this is the best I've felt for two years. I'd like to tell her a joke; she needs a laugh. I could tell her a story such as the one I over-heard last night when two nurses were in here cleaning the body up. They were laughing about a doctor who thinks he's God's gift to women. Well, it seems that when one of the nurses experienced the doctor's gift, she discovered that it was child-sized.*

I'm hovering close to the ceiling on the other side of the bed when Amina, my young African-American nurse comes in. She's a sweetheart. As I usually do when she comes in, I drop down to the level of the body so I can watch her eyes—so kind and peaceful. I love this girl.

After giving Mom a big smile, she wanders around the room touching various knobs and making notes in a folder. She replaces an IV bag, then stands behind Mom rubbing her shoulders.

"They told me today that it's time to let her go," Mom says, her voice cracking. "Even if she comes out of the coma, the cancer will take her immediately—or the cancer could take her before she comes out of the coma. I don't know what to do."

"You should go get some rest, Mrs. Whittaker. It's after nine."

> *Yes, Mom; go get some sleep. It's depressing watching you sit here all day.*

"I'll just stay a few more minutes."

Amina gives Mom's shoulders a final squeeze and a pat before moving on to the next room.

I drift up to the ceiling and look down.

> *I don't know why I hang around the ceiling. ... Maybe so I'm not in the way. Isn't that a laugh?*

Mom is looking down at her hand that's holding my hand—my body's hand. I move down so I can read the expression in her eyes. I hover a few inches above our hands looking up at her.

> *Jesus! There's so much grief in her eyes. It's like she's the one dying. ... I love you, Mom. Can you feel it? Can you feel how sorry I am that I didn't do anything worthwhile with my life? I never gave you grandkids. I would give every cell in my body if I could only give you something that would bring you some joy after I die. Oh God! She's crying again.*

> *Whoa! ...*

> *I'm inside her thoughts. ... I think. ... How the hell did that happen? I can feel her grief. I mean, really feel her grief. A moment ago I wasn't feeling anything ... well maybe a little bliss from being free of all the cancer pain ... and now, it's like sadness on top of sadness, like a ... I don't know what. ... How can she live this way?*

> *I was wrong; it's not really her thoughts. It's ... what ... her emotions or something?*

> *It's not just about me dying; she's feeling Lauren running off with Jeff to California; she's feeling Dad divorcing her; she's feeling all the pain that led to his leaving. She's feeling that her life meant nothing at all.*

I had no idea Mom felt this badly about her life. I thought she got over Dad and Lauren years ago. She hasn't talked about them for years.

I've got to do something about this.

I'm trying to focus on her grief. I don't know if it will do any good. She's feeling that she's wasted her life. She's only got me and I'm about to leave her. She's feeling emptiness. I'm attempting to hold onto my love for her and her grief as a single thought.

Mom is crying again, not the quiet tears that I've seen over the last few weeks since my fall. She's blubbering. It feels connected to the love that I'm feeling for her. She rests her head on the edge of the bed and seems to be emptying all her grief into her tears.

Mom is feeling my love; I'm pretty sure of it. We are somehow connected in a two-way channel. I'm feeling her grief while she's feeling my love. The more love I send her, the louder she cries.

How did I do that?

Now I'm feeling all her emotions, not just the grief but also the love that I'm sending through the channel that has opened between us.

I'll let this flow for a while. ... This is nice. ... I can feel the love passing to Mom, and I can feel when she feels loved, then I can sense her reaction coming back through the channel. The more I love her, the more comes back.

Amina walks in, then stands at Mom's right shoulder, looking down on the back of Mom's head which hasn't moved. She bends over, putting her right hand on top of Mom's right, the hand that's holding mine. She's rubbing Mom's shoulders with her left.

I should have been a nurse. These women are

incredible. Love you, Amina! ... Big hug!

From the ceiling all I can see is the top of Mom's head. I move down, just above the hands, so I can see Amina's face.

I wonder if I can wander into Amina's conscious-ness if I focus on how grateful I am for what she's done for Mom and me.

Yikes! ... I guess so. That was easy.

Now I'm feeling her emotions. This must be what they mean when they talk about compassion. She's really touched by Mom's suffering—actually feeling the pain, not simply understanding it intel-lectually. Is she able to do this all the time? With all the patients? God, she must be exhausted at the end of a shift.

I can feel her compassion but also the hurts, the residue of daily brushes with racism and sexism, the worries over her little boy left in a daycare facility that isn't quite as well run as she would have liked.

Am I reading her thoughts? ... No ... It's not that. It's more like her soul or spirit, something under the thoughts. ... Wow!

I feel stronger as I absorb her energy. I'm not trying to move anything through the channel in her direction.

What's going on? ... As soon as I had the thought that nothing was going in her direction, some-thing started slipping to her from me. I'm sensing both her emotions and, maybe, my gratitude flowing to her?

Amina is smiling. There's a tear running down the right side of her nose. She's wiping it away with her fingers, still smiling.

This is really cool! I made her smile. I wish I could give her that hug.

Amina turns away; I feel the link between us break. She walks over to the cabinets, pulls two tissues from a dispenser. After she blows her nose and dabs her eyes, she walks out. ... I can hear her talking to someone at the nurses' station in the hall.

I'm slipping back into Mom's consciousness. It gets easier each time. She really feels miserable. I've never felt this level of misery, not even during chemotherapy. Tomorrow, I'll see if I can get her to go home earlier—by three o'clock. She can miss the traffic, have a nice dinner and take a nap in front of the TV.

I'll have to play around with this psychic stuff. I'm still not sure how I do it. It is something like—I'm feeling the other person's feelings, then there's an intention to go beyond the feelings, like the feelings are floating on the surface of a lake, so I exhale, then allow myself to sink below that surface. I'm not aware of time exactly, only a gentle intention. Then suddenly—poof; there I am—I just know that I'm connected to them.

Mom is still crying softly. I want to speak to her, to say, "Mom, go home." but I know that won't work. I'm sending her love and appreciation. The channel seems to open. I send her the thought that I will be stable tonight—no way am I dying before she can get back here tomorrow. I send her gratitude wrapped with the idea that she deserves a night off. I love you, Mom.

Damn! Where'd she go? The room's empty. Where did I go just then? Time is a bit unstable in this ... this thing I'm doing—whatever the hell it is. The clock says nine-thirty. It's dark out. It must have worked. But I must have jumped forward in time, or maybe I dozed off. Can I doze off while in a coma? I don't know what's going on.

There are some loud voices in the hall. Amina is getting chewed out by the head nurse right outside my door. She's saying the old man next door didn't get his eight o'clock heart medication for some reason. The head nurse is really pissed. This will go on a report, she says; there will be a black mark at the group's next evaluation, so she'll see that there's a black mark in Amina's file.

Amina comes back in to change the urinary catheter on my body. She pulls down the covers and pushes the gown up. I move down to my crotch. *That's a strange thing to say, isn't it?* From down there I'm looking up her arms to her face. She's shaken. I can see the worry.

I move into her with all the thankfulness I can muster. I mean—here she is working in my crotch, changing the plastic tubes—not a glamorous job. ... It can't be too pleasant either; I haven't had a real bath in over a week. She's focused on what she's doing; the chewing out by the RN has slipped way down on her list of concerns.

> *Perhaps I can help her out. A few minutes ago I jumped forward in time—or I think I did—so I might be able to move back in time, so she doesn't get chewed out. Maybe instead of only being an observer, I can give people some new thoughts.*
>
> *I'll use the feelings-as-a-lake trick again. ... Some intention. ... Some love. ... A nudge back in time to seven forty-five. ... A thought about Amina giving Mr. Whatever his heart medication ...*

OK! ... I felt something change. ... It's nine-forty. She's still here, straightening the bed. She arranges my hair, tucks it behind my ear. She puts some cream on my dry lips. *Love you!* She looks tired but now she's more relaxed. She checks my monitors once more and leaves. I believe it worked; I don't think she forgot his meds.

The room is empty. I'm at the ceiling looking down on the inert body in the bed.

> *It would be cool if I could do this stuff at a distance. I can't always be looking at someone's face. I'll try to check on Mom at her apartment.*

I'm focusing on Mom, attempting to connect by feeling love for her, feeling grateful ... feeling grateful. ... No, it's not working.

> *I'm such a dummy! I can be wherever I want. I've been moving around the room all day—ceiling to hands, to crotch, to ceiling. What's keeping me in the hospital?*

I wander out to the nurses' station. There are only two people there, the head nurse and another woman I haven't seen before. I'm at the head nurse's keyboard looking up at her. She's in her early forties, pretty, with dyed blond hair.

> *That dye job needs to be touched up soon.*

She seems nice. It's easy enough to feel apprecia-tive. Here she is, taking care of us at ten o'clock at night. She wears a wedding ring and a big diamond engagement ring. Her husband and kids are probably at home wondering what it would be like to have a mother with a day job.

I slip inside.

She is doing OK, just stressed about the needs of the dozen patients who are spending the night in the ICU. I don't feel any worries about missing meds. I give her a spiritual hug and leave her.

I'm wondering how to get to Mom's apartment. It

was simple enough to get from my bed to the nurses' station. That was really just intention. It seemed slow, but I don't think it has to be.

I create some intention to be down on the sidewalk in front of the hospital. ... I'm there.

I think about Mom's apartment. ... I'm there.

> *This is fantastic! I should have put myself in a coma years ago! So where's Mom?*

A yellow glow is spilling into the hallway from her bedroom. Now I'm beside her bed. She fell asleep while reading a romance novel with a big beefy guy on the cover. It would be helpful to turn the light out for her, but I can't do that, I guess. I sit on the side of her bed. That's not right; I don't have a butt to sit on. I'm where my head would be if I had a butt to sit on the side of the bed.

I slip inside. It seems even easier when someone's asleep. She must be dreaming; the emotions are all over the place and changing quickly. I'll just give her some love and gratitude. ...

> *Was that a reaction? ... I believe so. I think I felt a flutter of happiness.*

She was, and is, a good mother. As I send her more appreciation, I can sense her heart being a bit lighter.

> *I probably didn't tell her I loved her enough. ... I told her, but not often. Could I be changing her dreams?*

I remember Mom always being angry, not always at Lauren or me, but angry at life. She would be making dinner; something would go wrong, then she'd burst. When I was little, she might yell at me, but later apologize. When I was a teenager—that was after Dad left us—I gave her a lot of grief and we'd both be yelling.

No apologies on either side. She didn't deserve what I put her through. That was my hippie phase; my life was sex, drugs and rock and roll, certainly not about caring for the needs of others.

I break the connection, then wander to the living room. I'm looking at the family pictures to remind me what is important to Mom at this point. She has one picture of her parents, but most of the pictures are of her and me or of me with my last boyfriend.

> *That's been a while.*

> *She probably has the pictures of my other boyfriends stuck in a drawer somewhere. Why didn't I ever marry one of them? ... Bill asked me twice. ... Too late now.*

She has a picture of Lauren, the one taken in 1980 when Lauren was a senior with her hair all piled up. She never wore her hair that way.

> *I've got to find Lauren. I remember how cute she was at five, six, seven. Always cuddling next to me. We adored each other so much then. Later we fought like cats and dogs.*

> *I'll see if I can find her—wherever she is. All I need is a little intention.*

* * *

Jesus! ... Don't ask me how I got here. I thought I'd be like Superman or something, flying across the country, across the plains, over the Rockies, then the Sierras. But that would have required knowing where I was going.

It wasn't that complicated. I was in Mom's living room. Some intention. ... Poof! ... And now I'm in Lauren's bathroom. Her place is old; knotty pine paneling, stained white porcelain sink; it's clean, but smells a bit musty.

I am shocked to see her suddenly in front of me, just getting out of the shower. She still looks good—trim, pretty. Her boobs are holding up better than mine. Imagine how shocked she'd be if she could see me. I can picture her screaming while falling backward into the shower curtain, dragging the curtain and the curtain rod down into the tub with her.

Boo! ... Hee! Hee!

I'm watching her get ready for bed, brushing her teeth, her hair. God, I love my little sister. She has a tattoo on her butt. What's that about?—some Chinese character. I can remember once when I was bending over exactly as she is now, brushing my teeth, when eight-year-old Lauren smacked my bare bottom and ran laughing down the hallway. If I had hands this would be a great time for payback.

She was so sweet as a little girl, trying to copy me in everything. She's five years younger than me. I guess I was a bad influence; as I became a hippy, she became one too. But she was much wilder.

I'll just wait for her in her bedroom. ... Hmm, ... seems like it's a studio, only a single room with a small kitchenette, a couch and a twin bed. Tidy. It smells of incense. I expected a mess, but I'm remembering her room at Mom's house in 1982 when she left. We all grow up.

Lots of books—some new-age stuff, some good novels, psychology texts, self-help.

Here she comes ...

The room is dark after she turns out the bathroom light. In the darkness before she turns on the lamp on the nightstand, I can see out the window, but there's nothing but pine trees, their silver outlines glistening in the moonlight. She sits on the side of the bed and relights the remainder of a joint that was resting on the edge of a tin ashtray. She takes two deep tokes, then tosses the roach into the ashtray where it burns itself out.

She pulls on a worn-out sleep-shirt. The hem is frayed and the armpits have holes. She gets into bed, then lays back on a pile of pillows. Her bedtime reading tonight is a vampire romance. I could never get into those things. I move next to her book to look up her arm. She seems to stare at me as she reads.

> *Now would be an even better time to yell "Boo." If I could just be a floating head with vampire fangs! I wonder if I could get her to piss herself like when we were kids. I've got to work on being able to do that. ... OK, time to get serious ...*

I'm enjoying staring at her. It's intense to be inches away from someone's eyes, looking deeply into them while they don't even know you're in the room. I'm trying to feel thankful for her, to send her love, but it's not working. She seems a stranger. I can't quite see her as the sweet little girl in 1967 or the unbelievably slutty teenager ten years later. I know it's her, but I'm looking at a fifty-year-old woman with wrinkles and leathery skin—and she's a blond at the moment, which is not her natural hair color.

After she left Cleveland with Jeff in 1982 there was one postcard from some small town in northern California, then nothing. If she'd kept in touch—an occasional photo—it might be easier for me to connect with her.

> *OK, Lauren, so you're a stranger. I need to be able to do this with strangers. What's the trick? ... I could become a Buddhist monk; they're supposed to have love and compassion for everyone. ... No,*

I don't have time for that. I'll be dead in a few weeks.

Gratitude. Gratitude. I'm not sending you gratitude; I think I'm sending you resentment, dammit. You left me with Mom, you little brat. ... And Dad left us before that. ... I was the one on the receiving end of Mom's bad moods for the last thirty years. ... Jesus! I could have used some help, you know?

You're so pretty. I was jealous of you for the last ten years we were together. You didn't know that, did you? I think I resented you back then too. Maybe I wanted to be the slut and you could have been the good daughter helping to keep Mom together.

She turns out the light, then turns to face the wall. I drift to the wall so I'm looking at her face, only inches away. She could feel my breath if I had any. She's even prettier in the soft blue glow that is coming through the window. In this light, I can imagine her at nineteen with smooth skin and light brown hair. She's falling asleep.

I remember, when she was seven or eight, smoothing her hair while she slept, lightly so it wouldn't wake her, pulling it back from her face and hooking it behind her ear. I'm thinking about the thirty years that we've lost, thirty years that we could have loved each other, and argued, and made holiday dinners together, and cried over romances gone wrong.

I'm still feeling resentment, dammit. I loved you and I'm resenting that I didn't have you to love after you and Jeff ran off. I'm even resenting that you put me in a position where I would resent you. It should have been love, dammit!

So why didn't you call?

Never mind; I know the answer to that. If I had

showed you any affection at all during our last ten years together, then you might have felt safe calling me. But I didn't show you any love, did I? I was bitter and pushy and complaining. Why would you call me?

OK, taking responsibility now ... I was the big sister; it was my job to help you after Dad left. I failed you, didn't I? You were only responding to my failure. You were running around with all those boys to get some validation that should have come from me. Yes, I can take responsibility for that.

I'm really sorry, Sweetheart. O God, I'm so sorry.

I'll focus on when she was eight. I was thirteen. I adored her then. I can see her at that age, especially in this light. I can be grateful that she was in my life, that she's still in my life. Sending joyful appreciation, appreciation, appreciation ...

Finally! It worked; I'm inside her.

So what do I do now? She's asleep; I could watch her dreams—doesn't sound very productive. ... I could wander through her memories of the last thirty years. Can I do that? I'll just keep sending her love and see what happens.

I'm only getting feelings, not really memories. I can feel that Jeff left her long ago. She romanced some men and some women—all gone. Loneliness. Unworthiness.

Why did she stay here?

She feels lost, her life wasted. Mom and I have that in common with her. I can feel laughter; she's had some good times, but those were long ago. The last ten years seem ... barren.

Is that the right word for this feeling?

It seems that she's in a commune, and has been this whole time. Now she works—garden, kitchen, ... children? Did she have children? No, I don't believe so. I think I could feel them if there were children of her own. She might be caring for other people's children.

I can feel her sex life—lots of sex with men and women. It seems she liked the women better. Hmm. ... But all that seems distant. The recent years just feel lonely.

There are scraps of memory about Mom and me. Embarrassment. Disapproval. She wanted to contact us, but she felt that we disapproved of her, of her sluttiness. ... Damn! ... We did, you know. We pushed her out. We never understood her.

> *How can I change this? I know I can move in time. I corrected Amina's medication mistake by backing up a few minutes. Can I back up thirty years? If I do, will I have what I need to make changes or will I be as useless to her as I was the first time?*

I'm still inside her. Well, I say I'm inside her, but it's really somewhere else. I'm where she and I are together in time and space. That's not very clear is it? It's like—there's something below our physical life, something more fundamental—like that psychic lake thing. Our physical bodies and our consciousness grow out of that thing somehow, and seem to be different things, but that's only seeming.

So I'm floating around in that something, and I can slip in one dimension and move through space, or slip in another dimension to move through time. Once I'm there, in that something, it only takes some intention to go wherever I want in time or space.

Yeah, I know; it still doesn't make sense. If you were

here, maybe you could describe it better. Does it make you feel weird when I talk to you directly? Hope not. You're here too, you know—in this time-space-lake thing. When I'm moving around in it, I sense your presence.

So I'm using intention to move back in time. I'm using her memories as a rough guide; the years in the commune are floating by, in reverse. The days are mostly the same. Lots of gardening in recent years. She likes it. Further back in time, there's lots of sex.

Finally, we reach her memories that are part of my memories: the last few years when she was at home, high school dances, homework, a play she was in during her junior year. I don't want to go back that far; I need to find a time a few months before she met Jeff Richards who drags her off to California—the bastard. ... I remember Darren Spenser asked her to the senior prom. That would be a good place to start.

Chapter 2

Wow! 1979. This is fantastic! I'm twenty-two! My body!—look at these hands—look at these boobs. I may have a new career selling this process. ... Well, probably not. ... If the process starts with being in a coma, it would be a hard sell.

I'M IN OUR OLD BEDROOM in Mom's first apartment, sitting on the side of my bed. Yellow walls, messy—especially Lauren's side. It's morning. Lauren is seventeen, asleep across the room in her bed. Jesus! This is real. I'm really here—in my old body.

This is great! I can move my hands. I can feel the blanket. Wait a sec! Is this a school day? What day of the week is it? I need to figure out what I'm supposed to do today. Right! I'm twenty-two and out of school, but I probably had a job.

I'm wearing a sleep-shirt and panties. I cross the room to sit on Lauren's bed. She's beautiful. It will be easy to send her love at this age. I nudge her elbow.

"What the fuck are you doing? Leave me alone," she swats at me and turns to face the wall.

"Do you have school today?"

"What? Are you crazy? It's Saturday. Leave me alone."

"Sorry. Sorry."

OK. She doesn't have school. Let me think. Let me think. ... Do I have a job to go to? Where's Mom?

I pull on some jeans and a sweatshirt, then go to the bathroom to pee and check my hair. It's been weeks since I could pee on a toilet—ah, the little pleasures of life. I look at myself in the bathroom mirror for a long while.

Look how young I was! —am, am! I could happily spend the day in here preening. Not a gray hair. No wrinkles, not even the creases between my boobs, or under them! Look at that! ... OK. ... Breakfast.

The apartment building was built in the fifties, part of a complex of six brick buildings with four, two bedroom units in each. The bedrooms are small and the closets a joke. The kitchens are tiny with worn Formica counter-tops, painted plywood cabinets and linoleum floors.

Mom is at the kitchen table drinking coffee and looking at the paper. She is fortyish but looks like a teenager to me.

"Morning, Sweetie," she says. "You sleep OK?"

"Fine thanks. How about yourself?"

I have to restrain myself from hugging and kissing her like a mad woman. Inside, I'm jumping up and down and screaming for joy. I pour myself a coffee and sit down across from her.

Stay cool ... stay cool ...

She smiles. Mom looks great. She's much younger than I am/was during the coma. I look at the paper; it's April 21, 1979. President Carter was attacked yesterday by a swamp rabbit while fishing in Georgia.

Damn rabbit probably thought he was a Yankee.

Dad divorced Mom in 1967 so he's long gone. She started working at the 7-Eleven in the mid-70s, so she'll probably be going to work soon. But what am I doing today?

"Mom, I know this is silly, but my mind is a complete blank. I can't remember what I'm supposed to do today. When I woke up, I didn't even know this was Saturday."

"Well, I suppose you'll be going to work, dear. You usually work on Saturdays."

And can you tell me where I work?

"Of course," I say. "Are you working today too?"

"Every Saturday. ... Are you all right?"

"I think I had some weird dreams that got me all turned around."

Mom nodded, then took another sip of coffee.

Where do I work? I remember it was some menial job. I didn't start working at the art gallery until after Lauren left.

I quickly eat a bowl of a miserable cereal, some sugary corn flakes, then take the coffee to my room. Lauren is still asleep.

I sit on the side of my bed to go through my purse looking for clues.

I hope this is my purse! If she wakes up and finds me in her purse ...

I find a pay-stub from the movie theater.

That's right! I remember that job. What else can I find in here? ...

My address book! So, who are my friends? There

must be fifty people in here. Who the hell are these people? It's amazing the details you forget. ...

Do I have plans for tonight?

Lauren stirs. She rolls over, opens her eyes for a second, then closes them again. She grimaces, then turns over to face the wall. I can't tell if she's going back to sleep or if she simply doesn't want to talk to me. Did we have a fight? I remember we fought quite often back then.

I find a work schedule in my purse. I'm due at the theater by eleven-thirty. I keep looking for clues about my 1979 life. I go through my address book again, trying to remember my friends. I examine all the scraps of paper, written in very neat handwriting.

When did I start writing sloppy?

I lie down on the bed with a novel to read until Lauren wakes up. I can't get over how my body feels. It's almost as if I don't have a body; it's so pain-free. I can't stop playing with my arms and legs; it's so easy to move them. For the last two or three years, every movement was an effort. It took a while to get out of bed; I felt every muscle groan as I attempted to lift the mass of me to a standing position. This body does whatever I ask without complaint.

About ten, Lauren sits up and runs her fingers through her hair. She looks like she might have had a wild night.

"There's coffee made; can I bring you a cup?"

"What the fuck do you want?"

"I want to bring you a coffee if you want one."

"OK. ... Sorry. ... Yeah, that would be great."

"How do you want it?"

"Black's fine."

When I return from the kitchen, she's coming out of the bathroom. I put the coffee on her nightstand. She slumps down on the bed, then picks up the cup. I'm sitting on my bed waiting to see if she wants to talk. She doesn't.

"Look," I say, "Can I talk to you a minute?"

"I guess, but not so loud."

"I want to really, really apologize for the last few years. I've been shitty to you. I don't know why. You didn't deserve it. I just want to say I'm sorry and I'll work on being a better person."

"Right. ... So what brought this on?"

"Maybe I'm simply growing up. I've been remembering how much we loved each other when we were little and how we would laugh and play together. Somehow that stopped. I think it was all my fault and I feel really bad about it."

"I think it was your fault too."

Did I see a hint of a smile?

"I've been taking you for granted," I say. "I was too wrapped up in my own little life. I don't know. I want you to know that you and Mom are the most important people in my life. I love both of you and I don't ever want to hurt either of you again."

Lauren is looking at me as if she is trying to see some sign that I'm conning her.

"Look!" I tell her, "Any time I hurt your feelings or piss you off, I want you to tell me so I can change. I'm serious. From today I want things to be different."

"We'll see."

"You will. I promise. ... What are you doing today?"

"Just hanging out. I may go over to Dianne's this afternoon. She was talking about going to the movies."

"I've got to go to work soon. Maybe I'll see you there."

Lauren nods, then takes her coffee mug to the kitchen to get some breakfast. I stand looking into our tiny closet struggling to remember what I did at the theater and if there was some uniform I had to wear. The closet is only four feet wide, so each of us gets two feet. I remember the constant battle over who was taking up more than their share. I can get rid of some of these clothes. It's not as if I care how stylish I am.

I am looking at each piece of clothing, using them to piece together the memories of how I lived in 1979. This wandering around in my past is harder than I thought it would be. I have forgotten ninety percent of the details of my life.

I'm lucky; there are three uniform blouses with the name of the theater chain embroidered over the pocket. I remember being an assistant manager or something for six months. I lay a blouse on my bed, then go through the chest of drawers doing the same re-familiarization exercise.

I find a bundle of keys in my purse. One of them probably fits the back door of the theater. If I go in a bit early maybe I can remember what my duties are and find the names of the other employees.

I'm going to make an ass of myself.

I kiss Mom goodbye and walk outside for the first time since arriving in 1979. I'm shocked; it's The Twilight Zone except in color. In the driveway is my first car, a faded, red '71 Pinto. I remember buying it when I graduated from high school in 1975.

Am I still making payments on it? Do I have any other bills? I'll look through my checkbook later.

The Bijou theater is a large, single screen building on Superior Avenue. There are only seven of us working today. I wonder why they even need an assistant manager. After being on the job for an hour, it's clear that the seedy little man who owns and manages the place is drinking most of his profits, so he has me to keep things running smoothly while he naps in his office. Today we are showing a comedy double feature, *The Pink Panther Strikes Again* and *The Big Bus*.

*   ✳   ✳   ✳*

Just after midnight, I'm back home, lying in bed. It went OK at the theater today. I was able to remember most of my duties and the names of some of the employees. Fortunately everyone was there and did their jobs, so I didn't have much to do.

Mom is asleep. Lauren isn't home yet. I really want to be awake when she comes in, so I'm stretched out on my bed, reading some of *The Great Gatsby*, one of my favorites from high school.

Lauren staggers in a few minutes after one o'clock. She is stoned. I think I catch a whiff of semen as she takes off her clothes. I put the bookmark in place and roll over on my side facing her. She dumps her clothes in a pile next to her unmade bed, then puts on the sleep-shirt she wore last night. I wait for her to flop into bed and turn off her light before speaking.

"Did you have a good time tonight?" I ask.

A few seconds pass. ... "What?"

"Did you have a good time?"

She sighs. "Yeah, it was OK. A bunch of us were hanging out at Dianne's house."

"Anything interesting?"

"Darren Spenser asked me to the senior prom."

"That's cool. What did you tell him?"

"He's a dork. I told him I'd think about it, but I'm not going with him."

"Hmm ... Well, good night."

"'Night."

"I love you."

"What?"

"I said, I love you."

"Jesus! Don't get all *Waltons* on me. Go to sleep."

I can't fall asleep yet. It's this body—twenty-two years old! I feel as if I'm on an adrenaline high all the time. I'll let Lauren go to sleep before I connect with her.

I need to put in a good word for Darren Spenser; he becomes an important attorney in town. He eventually has a really large house and a Cadillac SUV. In his forties he has multiple homes or condos. If he takes her to the prom, they could end up together, then she won't go off with Jeff Richards.

Wild thoughts are running around in Lauren. It's strange connecting with someone who's stoned. There must have been an orgy over at Dianne's. Darren was there. I'll see if I can get her to dwell on him for a while. ...

> *Oh, I see, he wasn't so great. The sex was a bit brief—almost instantaneous.*

So while she's remembering almost having sex with

him, I'll simply add the idea that he's going to be rich and powerful. And good looking! He gets these sexy gray temples in his forties. Of course, she's probably more interested in sex at this point.

> *If I could only tweak her mind so she always found him more exciting than he really is. That would be a good trick, wouldn't it? But they call that witchcraft, don't they?*

> *I think I've messed with her mind enough for one night. Let's both get some sleep and I'll ask her about it tomorrow.*

*   *   *

It's almost dawn. The room is filled with blue light. I'm lying here watching Lauren sleep. My head's in a good place. I cherish her. I want the best for her. A channel opens easily to send her love. I'm not messing with her mind, only sending a spiritual hug. When she wakes up, I'll try acting on my feelings. I don't know how loving adult sisters are supposed to act; that's a new experience for me. It shouldn't be, but it is.

I get up to pee, then lie down again. Mom's still asleep so I read *Gatsby* while occasionally looking over at Lauren. I'm still sending her love, but the channel isn't open; it's just the normal sisterly affection that I should have been sending her for years.

Around eight I hear Mom trudging down the hall to the kitchen. I get up quietly and follow her. She brews a pot of coffee while I make toast. I have to catch myself; she seems like another little sister. I have to keep telling myself that I'm twenty-two and she's my forty-two-year-old mother.

We spend the next two hours together being domestic.

She reads the paper while I clean the kitchen. Nothing is really dirty; I'm enjoying being near her. So I polish the refrigerator and the handles at the sink. I take a toothpick and remove the fine line of grunge where the porcelain sink meets the counter-top. She's telling me about interesting things in the paper while I polish. I'm happy to hear what was important to her at forty-two.

Her biggest worry is the economy. She's pissed at Jimmy Carter who she blames for inflation. She worries about her job. Being a cashier at 7-Eleven is not a secure position. The number of cashiers goes up and down with the volume of business. The volume is down at the moment. The manager hasn't said anything, but Mom frets over having to look for another job.

When she stops talking, I open a channel to her. I find that it is a little more difficult to maintain the connection with my eyes open.

> Mom is worrying about Lauren and the crowd she runs with. She worries about me finding a husband. Her thoughts seem to be all worries— no friends, no hobbies, no plans—just plodding through the calendar at the mercy of fate.

> When am I going to find a man? I'm twenty-two; I could start looking. It doesn't feel right though. Why is that?

> Well, for one thing, I'm fifty-five and dying. I'm just visiting in this body. I don't believe I can handle any more complications.

I sit down at the table with her. I pick up a section of the paper she's already read.

"Mom, I think you need a girlfriend to hang out with. Do you have anyone like that?"

"What? ... Well, there's ... not a girlfriend exactly ..."

"What about your old girlfriends from high school? Do you stay in touch?"

"Most of them moved away. Doris still lives in the city, but she's turned out a little too right-wing for my taste."

"You and Dad used to go to parties; do you see any of those people?"

"Well ... you know ... they were mostly your father's friends. I always felt ... I always felt beneath them. They were from the wealthier families. I was the poor girl that your father married. They thought he married beneath himself. ... He probably did."

"Maybe you and I should go out sometime, have a few beers. We could meet some of the local women who aren't in the country club set."

"Maybe we should."

Lauren shuffles into the kitchen about eleven, mumbles something unintelligible that sounded as if it might have been pleasant.

"Good morning, Sweetheart," says Mom while Lauren pours herself a coffee.

Lauren sits down at the table, then notices me smiling at her. This seems to confuse her.

"What are you smiling at?" she snaps.

"Believe it or not, I'm really delighted being here with you and Mom."

She's not buying this at all. She wrinkles her nose at me as if to say, *You're only saying that for Mom's benefit. What are you really after?*

I don't expect Lauren to get it. She can't visualize our

elderly mother holding my hand in 2012, crying at my deathbed. I really am feeling a burst of love for both of them.

"Last night you said that Darren asked you to the prom. Are you still going to turn him down?"

"Yeah, ... I don't know. ... Maybe I'll say yes for now, and see if someone better comes along."

> *I'll work on her again tonight—try to make Darren seem like a better date than whoever else she has in mind.*

I kiss Mom on the temple, give Lauren a quick shoulder squeeze, then shower and dress for work.

* * *

I return from the theater at ten-thirty that night. Mom has fallen asleep on the couch, watching TV. I nudge her awake then hold her hand as she rises to go to bed. I'm still feeling as if I'm her older sister.

Lauren is in bed reading an English textbook and making notes.

"Hey," she says with a hint of a smile as I enter our room.

"I hope you had a great day," I tell her as I start to undress.

> *That sounded lame. I don't know what to say to her. I want to keep saying how much I love her, how beautiful she is, how smart she is. None of that can be said; she'd think I was nuts.*

"Yeah, it was OK."

I get ready for bed, then brush my teeth. When I return, I pick up Gatsby and pretend to read it. I'm really opening a channel to her; it opens easily.

She's focused on her studies. I slip past her thoughts of English literature and find her impressions of Darren. She had sex with him last night. It was passable, but she had two guys who were more energetic; one of them really rang her bells. However, she found that guy dumb and insensitive, so her interest in him is waning. Darren seems a warm glow.

I'm sending her the same messages as last night— Darren as a good provider, distinguished attorney, gray temples, really handsome.

> *I could hang out in this time-line for a few years to see what happens with Darren, but I'm not patient enough, or confident enough, to do that. I also don't know whether dying in 2018 is going to make me disappear from this time-branch in a few days. I have no idea how all this works, so I'll just fast forward ten years to see how this Darren thing turns out.*

Chapter 3

So, is this 1989? What month? It's early morning.

I'M LYING IN MY ROOM in Mom's apartment. *The Great Gatsby* isn't on my nightstand, but I see it on the shelf. The walls are now painted a powder blue; they were a pale yellow when Lauren and I shared the room. Her bed is gone; in its place there's a small computer desk with an old Macintosh computer. All the teenage decorations are gone; there are no posters of rock bands or movie idols, only two abstract prints that look as if they might be my current taste.

Should I be rushing off to work at the art gallery? I know I'm not working at the theater any more. That's not true. In my original time-line, I would have left that job nine years ago, but now—who knows? Maybe I'm the drunken owner hanging out in her office while the young assistant manager runs everything.

Jumping around in time is such a pain. Well ... only because I don't want to make a fool of myself. I could simply go to the art gallery and say, "Hi, whoever you are, do I work here? What are my hours? Are you my boss or am I yours? Please don't fire me!"

I dig through my purse looking for clues. There's a pay-stub from the art gallery so possibly my career is intact. I can't tell what day it is today. I take a quick shower. The house seems chilly, so I dress in a sweat-suit.

> *What season is it? I can't tell. There are leaves on the trees—so spring? Summer?*

Mom is in the kitchen scrambling some eggs as I walk in. I hug her shoulders and pour a coffee. There's a newspaper on the kitchen table.

"Is this today's paper?"

"Umm ... No, that's yesterday's. The kid hasn't delivered the paper yet."

It's Tuesday's paper, July 18, 1989.

> *Jeez, it should be warmer in here. She must have kept the air conditioner running overnight.*

"It's so cold in here, Mom."

"I know. Ever since I went through the change, I'm so hot all the time. Sorry."

"It's OK."

> *Ah! Hot flashes—I'm happily taking a thirty year break from them at the moment.*

> *Am I late for work? The kitchen clock says eight-fifteen. I usually went into the gallery about nine, so we could open at ten. There's no time to chat this morning.*

I eat the scrambled eggs, then return to the bedroom to dress for work. All the clothes in my closet look wrong. I can't get my head to think in terms of 1989 styles. We were always conservative at the gallery so I choose a white blouse and a black skirt. A single strand of pearls should work. I throw a scarf and more jewelry in my purse so I can make some adjustments if needed.

In the driveway sits a Plymouth Reliant, my first new car. I settle into its plastic seats, then start the engine. The odometer says twenty thousand miles, so it should be more reliable than the old Pinto. It's almost out of gas, so I stop at a service station a few blocks from the gallery.

A kid with "Bobbie" in the white oval above the pocket of his blue uniform shirt comes out to pump the gas. He starts the tank filling, then asks if the oil is OK. I tell him I don't know. He tells me to pop the hood, but I don't know how to do that. He shakes his head indicating that I'm a ditsy broad, then reaches through the window to pull the release handle next to the door.

Bobbie tells me the oil is OK and I owe him sixteen seventy-five for the gas. For a moment I think I'd like to stay at a time where a gallon of gas is only a buck twenty, then I remember that I'm probably making five bucks an hour to pay for it.

I park in the alley behind the gallery, glancing around for menacing characters before leaving the car. There are plenty of places for a mugger to hide. The gallery is one of six businesses that face Euclid Avenue. On the other side of the alley are old row-houses with dilapidated garages that look as if they could be used as a set for a movie about a serial killer who prefers to torture his victims before the final act.

As I walk in, I see that we are between shows. Paintings are leaning against walls. Unopened boxes are stacked in the center of the room. Cheryl, the gallery owner, wearing jeans and a T-shirt is prying open a crate. It's wonderful to see her twenty years younger than she was when I quit last year.

> *Jeez! "Last year" doesn't have much meaning when I'm jumping around in time like this; I mean 2017—when I stopped working because the chemo*

got to be too much for me.

She frowns and reminds me that I was supposed to dress casually so we could take down the old paintings and redo one of the rooms for a sculpture show that opens this weekend. I apologize and tell her that I'll change during lunch so we can do the dirty work in the afternoon. She says it works for her.

During lunch at home, I take advantage of having the house to myself. I wander through the living room, nibbling on a sandwich, searching for clues about Lauren. In the top drawer of the credenza, I find an album of wedding photos and snapshots of Lauren and Darren in front of an expensive house and two different luxury cars.

> *Are they still together? I'll talk to Mom tonight. What would be a good question that wouldn't make me sound as if I've been asleep for ten years?*

* * *

I'm watching *Night Court* when Mom comes home a little after eight.

> *I know, I know—not the greatest sitcom ever made. It's only that I like Markie Post. Besides, watching it in 1989 with a 2012 brain, there is a level of absurdity in the show that matches the craziness in my own life. ... Why am I explaining this to you?*

"You want a beer?" Mom yells from the kitchen.

"Sure. Thanks."

"Can we watch *Anything But Love*?" she asks, as she hands me the can. "I like Jamie Lee Curtis."

"Sure."

I switch the channel. There's a commercial for laundry soap. I sip my beer until the next commercial break.

"Mom, what have you heard from Lauren recently?"

"I haven't heard from her for over a month."

"Do you think she's happy?"

"As far as I know, but she doesn't really talk about feelings with me. She likes to talk about the things they're buying. The last thing was a big houseboat that they're going to keep at the lake—sort of a getaway cabin."

"How long have they been married? I can't remember the year."

"Three. No, almost four; they were married in the fall of '85."

I excuse myself to go to my room. I kiss Mom on the forehead, rub her shoulders for a few seconds, then head down the hall.

I get ready for bed, find a novel that I could reread, then lie down to visit Lauren. I put the open novel on my belly so it would look as if I fell asleep reading should Mom check on me.

Lauren is twenty-seven at the moment, living some-where nearby. I focus on her, on my feelings for her, on how glad I am that she's my sister.

It only takes a few seconds to connect with her.

She's with several people—a party? Wednesday night? An orgy? Probably not. She feels bored. Some kind of meeting? I'm looking for feelings about Darren. ... I'm getting resentment. ... Jesus! This is some kind of church meeting!

Lauren at a church meeting? I must be in some

twisted alternate universe. I'll come back to her later after she's home.

I break the connection and read my book for a few hours—*Love In The Time Of Cholera,* by Gabriel Garcia Marquez. It's not bad, even in translation.

I wake up at ten-thirty. I guess the book put me to sleep. I connect to Lauren again.

She's with Darren at home, getting ready for bed. She's conflicted. I feel her appreciation of their lifestyle, but at the same time, she resents being controlled. I don't sense any love for him. Is she pushing back against his control? I think so, but I'm not sure. I'll have to find a way to talk to her. I hope our relationship for the last ten years has been better than before. I send her some love before breaking the connection.

* * *

On Thursday, I call her home number at nine when I get to the gallery. I'm by myself; Cheryl said she would stop by the bank on her way to work. I'm nervous; I have no idea if Lauren wants to talk to me.

"Hello."

"Lauren. Hi, it's Cailyn."

"Oh! Hi. It's been a while."

She sounds as if she's glad to hear from me!

"Yes, it has. I was hoping you were free for lunch or dinner sometime soon. I'd like to catch up—see how you are."

"Well, … OK, yeah, where would you like to meet?"

"Could you meet me for lunch today at the coffee

shop next to the gallery? When is good for you?"

"Sorry, I can't today; there's a meeting at church all day. I could meet you there tomorrow at one."

*   *   *

The next day I'm sitting in a booth sipping tea when Lauren walks in, smiles, then sits down across from me.

She really looks good—dressed for success. There is nothing left of the sloppy, slutty teenager.

"You look great," I tell her. "Your hair is fabulous."

"Thanks, ... but it's been this way for at least a year." She gives me a funny look that tells me I've seen this hair style a few times.

"Maybe it's the light."

The waitress takes her drink order: a coffee.

"So what have you been up to lately?" I ask.

"Well, let's see. We recently finished vacation Bible school at our church. Since I didn't have a job, I got roped into helping with the preschool kids."

"I never pictured you as a Sunday school kind of person."

"Jesus! Me neither! With Darren, it's all about his business, so we belong to the biggest Baptist church in town, and he insists that we be very active. He says it's a great source of clients. He does estate and tax law so all the old farts come to him."

"I never thought of that. I bet that's true."

"What's new with you?"

We pause while the waitress brings Lauren's coffee and takes our food orders.

"What's new with me? ... We have a new show opening at the gallery this Saturday. You and Darren could drop by. There are some really creative sculptures by three artists."

"We have a party on Saturday night. ... There's *always* a party on Saturday night."

I'm sensing more of her unhappiness. I'm getting this from her face, not from a psychic connection.

"Lauren, tell me if this is too personal, but are you happy with Darren?"

She looks down at her coffee for several seconds, then looks me in the eye.

"It's hard to say. We have a great life—lots of things happening—good things. We're traveling as much as I'd want to travel. Plenty of friends. ... There's something not quite right," she stares out the window for a while at the traffic passing by, then, turning back to me, she continues. "He controls every aspect of our lives. He asks my opinion, at least, but in the end he makes all the decisions."

"Part of that's the religion, right? Aren't Baptist men the heads of their families."

"Well, that's true, but we don't believe the crap the church preaches. It's just Darren, you know. He has his plan, and works his plan, bulldozing every obstacle out of the way. He's incredibly driven."

"I was thinking when you walked in that you were the picture of success. That's great, but when we were teenagers, we were both more like hippies than conservative business types. I wonder if that was the real us or is this the real us?" I gestured toward my own business clothes.

"I'm happier than I was then. I'm less angry. ... But I haven't really found myself yet. This," indicating her smart gray suit, "doesn't seem like the real me."

"Do you know what you'd prefer to be doing?"

"I've tried imagining something more fulfilling, but it's too hard to think outside of Darren's plan. My only job is to support his career. If I wanted to open a shop, or go back to school, or learn to sing—anything—it would have to be something that would bring in more clients. It wouldn't be enough for me to make a little money at something I enjoy."

We both are lost in thought for a few minutes, nibbling on our meals. I decide to change the subject.

"In the last few years, I've been really sad about the years we wasted being angry with each other. I hope we're growing close like we were before we were teenagers."

"I think we *have* been growing closer." She smiles, then sips her coffee. "You've been great ever since ... well, for several years, anyway."

The waitress brings our food. While we eat, I try to connect with her, but I can't do that and talk to her at the same time. We share some small talk over the meal, then she has to run somewhere, and I have to get back to the gallery. As we part, I tell her I'll call next week.

That night as I lay in bed, I decide to move forward in time. I don't want to stay with her in this time-line, nudging her this way and that. It doesn't feel right to manipulate her. I've screwed up my own life; I can't risk screwing up hers. So I move ahead another ten years to take a peek.

* * *

This should be 1999, but where the hell am I?

A digital clock glowing in the darkness says 2:17. I don't recognize anything. Someone warm and nude is in my bed. That's a surprise. ... Someone who shaves their legs. Oh my! It's not a guy—even more of a surprise. I sit up. No clothes on me either. My eyes are slowly adjusting to the faint moonlight coming through the bedroom window.

> *It's Cheryl. I didn't know she was gay. ... For that matter, I didn't know I was either. ... Oh, what the hell, it's only for one time branch.*

> *Maybe this is the reason I never married ...*

I lay down on my back. This rouses Cheryl. She cuddles up and, emitting little sighs of pleasure, kisses me on the shoulder.

> *God! I hate jumping forward in time. Although, the morning will be interesting.*

Slightly distracted by Cheryl's large breast resting on my arm—is she still my boss?—I connect with Lauren.

> *Waves of unhappiness, worry. What's going on with her? Emotions about Darren feel like anger. It seems they've broken up a year ago. How's her self-worth? ... Oh! I see; Darren dumped her for someone else. Damn!*

> *Her self-worth is in the toilet. She's thirty-seven, feeling over the hill. She never developed a career of her own so now she's contemplating working at the 7-Eleven like Mom. One minute she's the glitzy wife of a successful attorney, and the next she's shopping at Walmart.*

Damn! I've got to go back in time again. There was another nice guy who liked Lauren before the party where she met Darren. But before I leave this time-line, I think I'll have some laughs.

Connecting with Darren is taking me a while. It's easy with Mom or Lauren because I love them and that helps open the channel. Darren's channel feels as if it's a clogged kitchen drain, but I'm gradually getting through the sludge.

> *Oh good! This is what I was hoping for—Darren and his new squeeze are going at it. Now I just need to distract him. Hee! Hee!*

> *How about some pictures of drowning kittens, big boy? ...*

> *What? You're not stopping?*

> *Darren! Drowning kittens! You creep! How can you hump away while kittens are fighting for air? Look at those sweet, frightened little faces. You callous bastard!*

> *OK, how about a sweaty, dirty homeless guy who's coming on to you? Kiss, kiss! He won't take no for an answer, will he? Now I've got your attention. He wants you, Darren. He wants you.*

> *Oops—Little Darren sort of plopped right out didn't he. Gonna get it hard again, man of steel? Switch to manual for a while, eh? ... No, that's not working, is it? Picture that homeless guy holding his raincoat open and blowing you air kisses; maybe that will help. ... No? ...Let's go back to the drowning kittens. ... Yes, I think it's time to give up too. ... I'm sure she'll understand.*

> *OK. Time to go. ... Back to 1979 ...*

Chapter 4

January 1979, I think. Morning. Six-ish. Yellow walls. Mom's apartment.

I NEED TO KNOW WHAT DAY IT IS, so I slip on my terry cloth robe and fuzzy slippers to shuffle down the short hallway to the kitchen. On the table is yesterday's newspaper—Wednesday, January the tenth. Mom must be asleep, but she'll be up in a few minutes, so I put the coffee on, then head to my bedroom.

I don't know what's worse, going back in time and losing whatever progress Lauren and I have made, or going forward to land in a whole new situation with no idea what's going on.

So I'm once again rooming with slutty Lauren. If only I could have brought the more mature Lauren back in time with me and, sort of, injected the improvements into this angry, beautiful sister of mine.

At least I know what she can become. Watching her sleep like this, so peaceful, it's easier and easier to love her. Maybe I should connect with her—see what's going on in her life. ...

No ...

I changed my mind; I'm going to simply be her sister for a few days. I need to get readjusted to this new time before I go messing with her mind. I need to love on her for a while.

I need to do the same with Mom. I owe her some love. In all this jumping around in time, I keep picturing her as the tired old woman crying at my bedside in 2012.

> *Knowing that I'm dying has advantages. I wouldn't recommend a death sentence to everyone, but I'm glad that I don't waste any time looking for work or hanging out in bars hoping to get seduced by a doctor who "normally doesn't go to places like this." All I have to worry about is being a good sister and daughter. Most of the things I fretted over in my original life have ceased to exist for me. Am I going to worry about an extra pound or a new wrinkle?*

I hear Mom stirring in her bathroom. I return to the kitchen to wait for her. I'm sipping my first cup of coffee when she comes in, her eyes half closed.

"My! ... You're up early."

"I feel good this morning. It felt as if I should be up moving around."

"Your sister still asleep?" asks Mom as she pours herself a cup.

"Soundly."

"I didn't get enough sleep. I think I'd sleep better if she wouldn't stay out so late, or if she was happier. She runs around at night, then lashes out at both of us during the day."

"Some of it's my fault," I tell her. "For the last five or six years, I've treated her as if she was an irritation. I'm so sorry about that."

I look down into my cup, but feel Mom searching my

face while she sips her coffee.

"We both screwed up," she says. "We should have made her feel special so she wouldn't ... well, you know. I believe she idolized you and compared herself to you, always feeling second-rate."

"Do you think it's too late?"

"I don't know. We have to try, I guess. It's hard when she's so angry, but maybe you and I can help each other find things to do or say that will make her feel as if we're on her side."

* * *

Mom and I were loving and supportive for several days. If anything, Lauren seemed angrier. Perhaps she thought we were faking it, playing some kind of twisted game with her. However, Mom seemed happier; working together to help Lauren seemed to be bringing us closer together.

Because I've returned to January 1979, all the wonderful progress Lauren and I made in the other time branches hasn't happened. I decide to have a talk with Lauren the next time I think she might be receptive.

* * *

Thursday night, about nine.

Lauren is sitting cross-legged on her bed, studying. I'm stretched out on my bed, reading. I turn on my side facing her. She looks as if she might be having trouble focusing.

"Can we talk for a few minutes?" I ask.

"About what?" she growls.

"Our relationship."

"What for?"

"I need to apologize to you."

"So, what have you done now?"

"You and I were really close until I was about thirteen. Then something changed in me, maybe puberty; I don't know. Anyway, I was a real shit for several years. Then when you got into your teens, it got even worse. We were both angry. You had a right to be mad at me. And I treated you as if you were the enemy ... really badly. I want to apologize for that."

"So why now?"

"I don't know, but I want you to know that you and Mom are the most important people in my life."

She looks at me as if I'm insane. "So, what do you want from me? It sounds like you're after something."

"Nothing."

"Bullshit! You treat me like crap for years and you expect us to be all sweetness and light?"

"OK. You're right. All I'm asking is that you stop expecting me to treat you like crap. Expect kindness from me. Test me. If I'm unkind, tell me."

"Look, this sounds like a con, but, yeah, I'll tell you when you're being a bitch."

"I think that's all I want for now."

"Deal!"

That last word was spit out. I'm seeing her anger. It's unpleasant, but I'm glad she can express it. I hope we can get it all out.

She lies down, turns to face the wall, then returns to her textbook. I turn on my back and open a channel to her. I want to send her the thought that I cherish her—try to erode her distrust a little.

It's so pleasant being in her consciousness without using my mind or hers, simply wandering between our spirits or souls or whatever this is. I can sense the tender relationship we had when we were small children, wallow in those feelings that are still there, in both of us, underneath the hurt. I'm glad to see that she feels them on some level, that those feelings are still part of her. One of the reasons she is so angry might be those good feelings have become a distant memory, buried under years of conflict. She could be grieving the loss of our relationship.

These memories of her as a child make my love for her expand. It seems to fill my body, then it envelops the whole room. Inside this joyful love, she's not just a seventeen-year-old girl; I see her at many ages, all at once. When Lauren was born she was like my personal, live doll. When she was old enough to talk, she became more of a person, later a friend. Because of the other time branches, now I can see her as a pleasant and responsible adult. As I lie here, it's wonderful to be able to experience all the layers of my feelings for her.

I never knew love could be this way. Before I got sick, love was only something to make me feel good. Boys or men would make me feel wanted, or give me a tingle; it wasn't about something flowing from me to another person. It was all about what was coming to me.

I was so selfish with everyone. Now I can see that, before my coma, when I loved her, it wasn't real; it was conditional. It was because she took care of me. If she hadn't, I might not have even liked her. I wasn't a good person.

Now, somewhere in 2018, I'm dying. Only Mom loves me. No one else wants someone who's days away from being a corpse. My days of romance, tingling breasts or genitals are over. What can Lauren, or anyone else, do for me unless they have a cure for cancer? Of course, at the moment, neither Mom nor Lauren knows I'm dying. And if I told them that I'm going to die in thirty years, I probably wouldn't get much sympathy.

While I've been examining my relationship with Lauren and Mom, I've been meandering through the relationships in Lauren's life. Whew! She is so looking for validation through sex. ... Way too often, my dear! ... We have to get her to pare down her sex partners before the AIDS epidemic hits in a few years.

I wonder if any of these boys she's screwing could give her real validation. ... It's not likely.

I'm tired. I send her a kiss on the cheek, then break the connection. She whips around to look at me, lying on my bed holding up a novel as if I'm reading it.

"What is it?" I ask.

"Nothing. ... Uh, ... I felt something touch me."

"I didn't see anything."

> *That was cool. I've never been able to do physical stuff before.*

She returns to her book. I consider kissing her again, but I decide that would be mean. Instead I walk to the side of her bed and rub both her shoulders for a few seconds. She stiffens.

"I'm going to the kitchen. Can I bring you anything?"

She turns to look at me, "No, thanks."

> *Did she smile? ... only for a split second? If she did, was it intentional?*

*   *   *

Two days later, it's early Saturday night. Lauren is getting ready for a party. I decide to go with her by connecting with her before she leaves, then hopefully staying with her throughout the evening. As she's getting dressed, I tell her that I'm going to take a nap. I lay down and watch her getting dressed for a few seconds until I feel the connection start. I close my eyes.

She's really excited. It's exhilarating to feel that, through her. I haven't felt any excitement in my life for quite a while.

Two girls pick her up in an old Corvair. The three of them are laughing as they drive away. I thought the distance might break the connection, but no, it seems to be working. I'm not listening to their chatter, just experiencing their elation through Lauren's emotions.

> *Whoa! I remember that feeling! They must be passing around a joint. This will be interesting.*

They arrive at the party. I'm going to stay below the surface of Lauren's mind; I don't want to share her sensory experience, only her emotions.

I feel her excitement ratchet up a notch. She's either drinking or smoking; I can't tell. Her thoughts are muddled—at least as I'm perceiving them. It seems she's becoming sexually excited. It's not as if someone is stimulating her directly; I think she's watching something.

> *I'll just take a peek. ...*

Oh, ... a naked couple is providing a bit of a show. I won't stay to watch; it could break the connection. I need to focus on Lauren, so I drop down to her emotions again.

Someone is gently touching between her legs—hmm, someone who knows what they're doing; she's about to explode. I wonder how I'm going to feel when she has an orgasm. ...

Ooh! I believe I'm about to find out.

The sex seems impersonal; I don't sense any emotional connection with whoever belongs to the hand. She's doing something in return. There are some outgoing emotions associated with her hand or mouth; I can't tell. I'm not going to look. It's not really important.

I'm looking for some romance—for Lauren to feel love for someone. The excitement is building. I sense people touching her and her touching others. She must be ready to climax, at least I would be, if I were that excited. She's going for the big O. There is so much stimulation; it is getting more aggressive and wild.

Oh my! ... I might have had a little orgasm myself, lying here alone in my bed at home, just from feeling her climax. ...

She is really enjoying this one. A wave of bliss is crashing from the top of her head to her toes, over and over. Wow! The kid knows how to cut loose.

A few minutes pass. She's calmer but not much. More drinking perhaps? I hope she doesn't get too plastered; I won't get any information from this exercise. She's starting to experience sex again. This is different; it feels like some guy is screwing her. It seems more violent, but a violence she's enjoying. ...

Then it changes; now other people are involved. The screwing energy is still there, but she's touching several people while they touch her.

This goes on for thirty minutes—nonstop stimulation. A few more big O's, but they don't do anything for me. I'm bored, impatient for it to end. Hopefully once she exhausts the sexual energy, there will be some emotions flowing to another person.

My boredom reminds me of Diane Keaton's line in "Annie Hall" when the Woody Allen character is having sex with her. She takes her consciousness out of the activity, then her consciousness tells Allen "While you two are doing that I'll just go over here and do some drawing."

I feel as if I need to read a magazine or something while Lauren's body finishes humping. I can't do that. I have to stay with her so I don't lose the connection.

She's experiencing the sex more as electricity than emotion; there's no romance only a tingling that waxes and wanes, from a mild buzz to shattering bolts of lightning. I'm a bit jealous; she's getting all her bells rung at once. I never had great orgasms, but then I never tried having sex with five people at the same time!

> *I'm exhausted by all this titillation. I think I'll go deeper into her. ...*
>
> *Hmm, ... this is surprising. ... I thought I'd be seeing a poor self-image. ... It's not that at all— more like a need for a tribe. Perhaps these kids have built a tribe around sex. This is what I needed to see: Lauren really needs to belong to something, and she hasn't been getting that from Mom and me. ... Dammit! She really needed me to give her a sense of family, but instead I gave her rejection and criticism. Mom was too absorbed in her own struggles; she didn't have time for Lauren. Mom was leaving it up to me to care for her emotionally. ... And I didn't care.*

I break the connection and open my eyes. I stare at

the white ceiling to let my emotions return to normal. I roll on my side and look at Lauren's rumpled bed.

I had hoped to find some guy at the party for her to fall in love with, a guy who could cherish her and build up her self-worth. Now I see that wouldn't work. She isn't looking for a knight in shining armor. She wants to be part of a group where she's respected as an equal contributor.

> *Where can I find an alternate tribe that's based on positive values, and how do I get her to accept them if I find one?*

* * *

Sunday morning.

Mom is at work. I'm in our room watching Lauren sleep while reading Passages, by Gail Sheehy. I close the book and my eyes to connect with her. It's simpler to connect with her while she's sleeping; there's less mental activity or chemicals to confuse me.

I sift through her feelings about last night. Beyond the drugs, booze and sex, there are some feelings for people. She had sex mostly with two particular men and five women. The men weren't important to her; the women were. There are some tender feelings. I'm surprised; it wasn't just about sex.

Two of the women seem really special to her. It feels romantic. There is also shame. She believes Mom and I would hate her if she told us she was gay.

Rather than be a matchmaker, I need to accept Lauren as part of our family tribe. A big part of making her feel accepted will be to let her know that if she wants to pursue a gay lifestyle, Mom and I will be supportive.

I've known several lesbians. They have something

of a tribe culture. That could be good for her. And it would keep her from getting AIDS, if we're lucky.

*   *   *

In the kitchen, early Monday morning, Mom and I are eating breakfast while Lauren sleeps.

"I've been doing a lot of thinking about Lauren," I say, over the top of my coffee cup.

Mom looks at me waiting for me to continue. She's not too chatty in the morning.

"First of all, I get the sense that Lauren is looking for a sense of community. She wants to be in a community with you and me, but we've … no … make that—I've rejected her. I feel horrible about how I've treated her for the last several years. When I started thinking about this, I thought she was rejecting us, but now I believe we're rejecting her."

"How can you say I'm rejecting her?" Mom's anger flared.

"OK. Sorry, I take it back. I've been rejecting her, but maybe you haven't found a way of reaching out to make her feel accepted. I don't mean that we're pushing her out on purpose. I'm talking about the way it feels to her."

"How do you know how she feels?"

That's a good question.

"I'm praying to be led to a way to help her, Mom. It's just the way I feel when I pray about it."

"OK, … if that's true, how do we change it?"

"There's another thing. … I ran into someone who knows Lauren, who has been to some of the parties that Lauren goes to. Lauren is bisexual, and it might be that she's more gay than straight. We need to find a way to show her that it would be OK if she decided to live a gay lifestyle."

"It is not OK if she's gay."

"Mom, think about it. Is that really how you feel? Is that really the message we want to send her?"

Mom turns away; she gets up to pour herself another cup, adds milk and sugar, then stands at the kitchen window while stirring the coffee. She watches the first few cars leave the parking lot, taking their owners to work.

"No, it's not how I feel," she says, then, after a pause, "but I do want a normal life for her. I want her to have children who have an attentive father to help look out for them."

"If that would make her happy—if she wants a husband. ... Perhaps two gay women in a stable relationship might do a better job raising a child than a husband and wife who often fight. I'm sure some of Lauren's feelings come from Dad leaving. I believe kids need stability more than anything. Don't you?"

Mom sits down. She has tears welling, just on the verge of breaking loose and tumbling down her cheeks. She takes a paper napkin from the table and dabs at her eyes.

I continue, "I'm suggesting it would help Lauren feel that we were a loving family if we simply came out and told her that her sexual preference is up to her, that we'll love her whatever she chooses."

Mom is struggling with this. I know it's too early in the day for such a heavy conversation, but the alternative was to wait until she came home exhausted from being on her feet all day.

"You're right," she says. "We can't make choices for her. Our only choices are to reject her or support her."

Mom is loading up her purse, getting ready to leave for work when Lauren enters the kitchen. Without speaking Lauren pulls a bowl and a box of corn flakes from the cupboard. Mom stands by the door, car keys in hand, waiting for Lauren to finish pouring milk in the bowl. She goes over to Lauren, wraps her arms around her, then kisses her on the cheek. Lauren is trying, feebly, to pull away.

"Your sister and I have been talking about sexual preferences. I think she's trying to tell me that she's gay. Anyway, my dear, I want you both to know that I want you girls to be happy. Whoever you bring home, male or female, I'll be happy—if you are. Gotta run."

Where did she get the idea that I was gay?

Without another word she flies out the door. Lauren sits down at the table across from me with a spoonful of cereal poised at her mouth.

"So, you're gay?"

I shrug. There is a long pause while I take a sip of coffee and gather my thoughts.

"I've had some ... experiences," I tell her, remembering Cheryl's naked body next to me—twenty years from now. Time branches make telling your life story problematic.

She chuckles at my discomfort, "Care to share?"

"I ... I slept with someone once. There's not much to say. How about you?"

"Yeah, ... I prefer girls."

"I thought so. I don't know why—a vibe I guess. Is there someone special?"

"No, not yet."

The idea of me being gay seems to have opened up some possibilities for her to relate to me. Even though I'm not gay, it's best to let her think that I might be. Hell, maybe I am. It doesn't make much difference what I call myself when I'm not sleeping with anyone.

"I was talking to Mom about both of us," I tell her. "I don't know if I'm gay or straight, but I wanted to make sure that Mom was cool with whatever."

"Why did you feel that you needed to tell her now? I mean—why not wait until you actually had a girl-friend before talking to her?"

"It was because of you. If I was right about you being gay, I wanted to make sure that you would never feel it was a problem. I want the three of us to be a real family, not three individuals who tolerate each other. I want you and me to love each other the way we did when you were five and I was ten."

"You're not thinking of anything kinky," she says while wrinkling her nose.

"Jesus, Lauren! Like when you were five, dummy. Except now we're adults and I can respect you as an adult, not treat you like a small child. Look—Dad left me too, and that made me angry. So I took my anger out on you. There was nothing fair about that; it was something a stupid young girl did to you. I hope, now that we're grown up, that we can get past everything, and be who we really are—who we are now."

Lauren appears to be considering all this as she

finishes her cereal, then washes her bowl in the sink. She sits back down with her coffee cup poised at her lips.

"Cailyn, I'm going to try to trust you, and to love you. Seriously, I will. But it means getting past all your bitchiness for the last ten years. I've got a lot to forgive you for."

My eyes are welling up now. I nod. I want to say I know, but my throat is dry. No sound comes out.

$$* \quad * \quad *$$

After Lauren leaves for school, I return to our room to lay down so I can slip forward in time to see how Lauren turns out in this time line.

At some point, I really need to work on patience!

I've found that I can fast-forward through her life like a DVD looking for the good parts. I do that, looking for happy moments.

She meets and falls in love with Kimberly in 1987 just as Kimberly finishes her masters in psychology. They move in together soon after. Kimberly encourages Lauren to go back to school. By 1991 Lauren has a B.S. is psychology and an admin job in the office of a psychiatrist friend.

Continuing to fast-forward, they seem content and stable. No wonder the marriage with Darren didn't go so well. Lauren seems to have found her tribe. They have a dozen women friends who all seem to care about each other. I'm also seeing plenty of friendly visits with Mom and me. Our relationship seems completely healed.

September 2001 passes with a negative bump as it

probably did for all Americans. After that, Kimberly and Lauren become increasingly involved with groups of women who are working to improve the lives of women and girls in the Middle East. By 2004 they are even more concerned when it becomes apparent that the lives of women in `Iraq are regressing by a thousand years because of the break-down of the old regime who, for all the horrible things they were doing to their political opponents, were at least encouraging more equal treatment of women.

By 2009 Kimberly and Lauren are in Afghanistan with three Persian-American women who speak Farsi, teaching literacy, basic arithmetic and hygiene to women in a small school in a mountainous tribal area north of Kabul. They are horrified at the degraded condition of the women and girls but excited about the progress their students are making.

Still fast-forwarding ... happy, happy, happy, then nothing.

I stop. Lauren is gone, or at least I can't find her. I slip backwards in time a few days. Still nothing. A few more days. She's back. Everything seems normal. I slip forward in time a few hours, a few more. That day seemed to go OK.

Just before dawn, men break into the school compound and drag all the women from their beds.

I break the connection. I can guess the end of the story. I lay in bed shaking with fear.

Perhaps I should be satisfied with this time branch. Lauren lived for forty-seven years. She found love with Kimberly. Mom and I had a good time with the two of them. Lauren had her tribe for twenty years.

I let the time branch roll on a few more years. I'm

still dying of cancer in 2018. When she finally gives up and has them turn off the life support, Mom is still alone, feeling as if her life amounted to nothing. Yes, Lauren and I loved her, but we were supposed to bury her, not the other way around.

Dammit! I've got to try again. I'll go back earlier.

Chapter 5

January 11, 1979. It's nine a.m.

I'M LAYING ON MY BED. The pillow is soaked with tears and feels cold. Lauren is in school. Mom is at work.

I have to force myself to focus on the live teenager who is probably doodling in a notebook during her first period class. She is not the naked, headless body, slaughtered by the Taliban a few minutes ago in my weird zig-zagging time-line.

I'm lying on my bed, eyes closed. I'm not doing anything psychic, just feeling my own thoughts. ... What is the right thing to do? ... I'm letting the events of the last few time branches wash over me.

What does Mom need? What does Lauren need? How much can I do?

I don't believe I can truly fix my little family from where I am, from 1979. It doesn't seem that I can nudge Lauren this way or that way and make this all come out OK. Even if I could, it doesn't feel like the right thing to do.

There's also something about my life that makes me die in 2018. It could have been something before Dad left, or perhaps something between 1967 and 1979.

I should return to the day that Dad left Mom. Not visit Mom or Lauren psychically but go there for real. I don't want Lauren to have to forgive me for being such a cruel sister; I need to change who I was. I want to start building our tribe in 1967, not struggle to fix the broken relationship as an adult.

Jesus! Do I really want to go back to being a child?

Chapter 6

Monday, June fifth, 1967, early morning.

I'M LYING IN BED looking at five-year-old Lauren across the room in her own bed. The bedclothes are a mess; she must have churned all night.

We are in the house that my parents purchased in 1959 when I was two. It's a brick Cape Cod, a pleasant, three bedroom on a half acre.

Dad moved out Saturday afternoon. Mom began crying earlier that day. She was still crying when he returned Sunday afternoon to pick up a few more things. I could hear her sobbing in her bedroom when I fell asleep last night around midnight.

Lauren has been crying too. She doesn't completely understand, but she knows something is seriously wrong because of the way Mom is acting. She and Mom are still asleep.

I go to the kitchen to make coffee. As it perks, I wash a few dishes from the last two days. We've only been snacking all weekend; no one felt like cooking or washing up.

I'm still the post-menopausal woman who's dying of cancer in 2018, but somehow I'm in this tiny, ten-year-old body. Look at me! I probably weigh eighty pounds. No boobs. No periods yet, as I recall.

How am I going to behave anything like a normal ten-year-old? In three or four years, am I going to get all giggly over boys? I doubt it. I did such a crummy job of puberty the first time, lashing out at Mom and torturing Lauren. Maybe this time I can enjoy having my hormones run wild.

> *Gee! I get to go through both puberty and meno-pause all over again! Wonderful! Not to mention another forty years of periods! O happy day!*

Mom shuffles into the kitchen, looking like hell. She slumps down at the table. I pour her a coffee, then put milk and sugar in it. When I put it on the table, she looks startled. I'm puzzled for a moment, then I realize that the first time I was ten, I never fixed her coffee.

> *Tonight I could fix her favorite drink, a whiskey sour. ... Hee, hee. ... Get a grip, Cailyn! You're not going to mess with her like that. ...*

I have to force myself to act like a child. There's so much that I know that children don't.

"Is the coffee the way you like it, Mom?"

"Yes, dear. It's perfect."

I stand next to her rubbing her shoulders with these tiny hands. She puts her left arm around my waist and hugs me hard. When she releases me, I continue rubbing her shoulders. I know how to give good shoulder massages, but these miniature fingers are almost useless.

While she sips her coffee, I start making toast. Again, she looks at me in amazement. But this is something I've seen her do a thousand times. She shouldn't be too shocked that I'm able to do it; what's shocking is that I am doing it rather than expecting her to wait on me.

I put the plate of toast, the butter and jelly on the table, then I stand behind her, hug her neck and kiss her on both cheeks with a loud, childish smack.

"I love you, Mom. We will be absolutely fine."

"Thank you sweetheart. I hope you're right."

"I'm a big girl, Mom. Up to now I've been letting you do everything around the house, but now it'll be different. I promise. I'll do as much as I can to take care of the house and help with Lauren."

She pulled a tissue from a box on the table, blew her nose and dabbed at her eyes.

I take a cup from the cupboard to pour myself a cup of coffee, then put it back when I realize that I don't drink coffee for a few more years. Besides, being in a ten-year-old body, I don't need a blast of caffeine to kick-start me in the morning.

I eat a piece of toast, then a bowl of cereal. As I'm putting my dishes in the sink, Lauren comes in looking about the same as Mom. I get down on my knees and give her a long hug, until she pushes me away to lay her chest across Mom's lap so her back can be rubbed. I put a bowl of cereal on the table for her, then go to check on the laundry baskets. Weekends were always our laundry days, but Mom had been too upset to do it. I start a load, then return to the kitchen.

"You started the laundry?" Mom asks.

"Yep."

"Did you separate the whites from the darks?"

"Yep," I smile.

"You know I prefer to wash my bras separately."

"Jeez, Mom, I've been watching you do it for years; I know how you do it."

I smile at her with a proud expression. She smiles back.

Mom will turn thirty-two this June. I'm fifty-five stuck in a prepubescent body. I will mess with her a bit.

> *If I'm going to have to go through the hell of child-hood and puberty all over again, I should be able to have a little fun with people. I look forward to torturing high school boys who are looking for a way to touch my tits in a movie theater. After I grow some, of course. I remember that was exciting in my original life; I'm sure it will be hilarious this time.*
>
> *OK, returning to reality ...*

"What are we going to do today, Mom?" I ask as I wash the dishes and place them in the rack to dry. She tilts her head as if thinking of an answer.

"Let's finish the laundry and clean the house this morning. After lunch we'll walk to the park."

"I'll finish the laundry and make the beds, if you can do the other stuff."

"That sounds great, sweetheart."

Later, while making the beds, a poem wanders into my mind. I decide that this time branch is a great opportunity to start a diary. I don't know why. I find a new composition book in my room, then sit on the side of my bed to jot the poem down.

On the first page I write:

5 June 1967

Mother is cleaning;
I hear her humming
that same song,
perhaps one of her mother's;
She never sings it though;
I wonder if her mother
hummed it too,
not knowing the words.

*   *   *

That night, at ten, I listen to Mom getting ready for bed, but I don't hear any crying. Lauren is in my bed, snuggled next to me. She seemed sad as I put her into her own bed earlier. I thought she would settle down, but a few minutes later, she asked to sleep with me.

After I turn off the light, there's only the bluish glow from the moon lighting up the white curtains. Lauren is quiet now. As I hold her, I can't help comparing this night to my original life when Dad left.

That first time, I was ten and feeling abandoned. God, how I acted out, splattering my anger onto Mom and Lauren. They had their own anger which they dumped back on me. We continued that cycle for ten years or so. This time, Dad's leaving isn't affecting me at all. I can probably nurture Mom and Lauren as if I'm the wise grandmother! ...

This is good.

During the night, Lauren wakes me up, crying in her

sleep. I hug her, kiss her forehead then whisper that I'm here—that she'll be OK. She whimpers a few more times, then falls asleep.

I try to calm myself, but I can't; I'm wide awake. I look at her face in the bluish light, remembering the fifty-year-old Lauren at the commune in California when my spirit first visited her.

> *This is what it should have been like the first time I lived through 1967 except I was too young and in so much pain. … I shouldn't beat myself up about who I was then. … I did my best.*

While I'm lying here, I could wander in Mom's head for a while …

I open a connection. It opens easily. Mostly Mom is feeling lost and scared about Dad leaving, but—there's something else—there's also a glimmer of something good. What's that about? It's not on the surface of her emotions; it's much deeper. I wonder if she's aware of it. I'll dig some more …

I feel some relief … something about Dad not controlling her anymore, not expecting her to be slaving at home all the time. … Maybe she wanted to divorce Dad for years but lacked the nerve. Did she want a career? … One day soon, I'll talk to her about her plans.

There's a feeling of unworthiness in Mom … something about being raised in a blue collar neighborhood by a father who worked in a factory where they made industrial glass parts. Also, it seems it was made worse by the tension between the sophistication my Dad expected of her and the plain Jane she saw in herself. I believe there was more conflict in Mom's relationship with her own father; she resented him for being so simple, and loved him for being so kind and generous. Part of her hates herself for the other part that resented him.

Jeez! Psychology can get a little complicated.

I fall back to sleep while I'm in Mom's consciousness. Lauren keeps waking me up every hour or so, but I'm able to drift off again.

*   *   *

Tuesday morning. The sun is just coming up.

Lauren is sleeping next to me, cuddling with her stuffed rabbit. We're lying in my bed while I do a little time-line planning.

Mom isn't working yet; she didn't start working until 1977 when Lauren is fifteen. She probably should get a job for her own self-esteem, but she doesn't really need to work since Dad treats us so well. He is, and will be, always regular with the alimony and child-support until 1980, when Lauren turns eighteen.

I remember he sold our house in 1968, then we moved into the apartment. Is that something I want to change? ... No, I remember that being OK. The apartment is in the same school district, so Lauren and I keep our old friends. Mom's friends will be close by, so maybe it doesn't matter.

Mom never remarried. I can work on that. I'll watch for a nice guy so I can put in a good word. I've lived in Cleveland my whole life so I know a few men who turn out OK. Of course there are the losers, those who married three or four times because no one could stand them for more than a few years.

Jeez! My mind is wandering all over the place. ...

What am I doing today?

What does a ten-year-old do on a summer day? I really don't know how to be a ten-year-old, or even a twenty-year-old. The first time I was ten, I probably spent this summer with some girl friends. ... Who were (are) my girlfriends? ... Well, I remember two, but there were other girls. I guess I'll wait for the others to call. How am I going to spend a day with little girls? I'll be climbing the walls—ready to go out with some friends for a few margaritas—like that's going to happen anytime soon!

A daily schedule for the summer: I'll help Mom with the housework every day in the mornings, then the afternoons will be for Lauren and my friends. I'll call my best friends later today, Pam and Lisa.

Does Lauren have friends? I don't remember; I'll have to check that out. She really needs friends her own age.

I hear Mom getting up.

I take my diary to the kitchen. As the coffee perks, I stand in the doorway between the kitchen and the hall, looking at the light coming through the glass in the front door. The coat hooks just inside the door catch my attention. I grab the diary and a pencil to write this down as I continue to look at the door:

6 June 1967

On that empty peg,
the one closest to the door,
hung his overcoat,
smelling of tobacco,
and aftershave;
Sometimes,
when I walk by,
I hear the rustle
when he put it on
that last time.

Chapter 7

Friday, June 9, 1967. Afternoon. Sunny.

MY FRIEND, PAM, AND I are in a small neighborhood park near our house. We are both bored. She was hoping we could watch some guys—guys our age—playing ball or frisbee. According to her strategy, we wouldn't be obvious; we would look off at an angle, watching them out of the corner of our eyes. Anyway, that was her plan, but there aren't any boys our age, only some high school guys with no shirts playing 2-on-2 basketball.

I wouldn't mind ogling these guys for a while.

Instead, we go to Pam's house, a fifties split level with lots of tired blond furniture. She suggests that we listen to records in her room. We lie on the floor with a small, pink and tan record player that only plays 45s. We spend most of our time changing records and sifting through the stack to choose the next one. I'm amazed at how work-intensive listening to music was in the dark ages before CDs and iPods.

As *Penny Lane* by the Beatles starts playing, she says, "Do you want to practice kissing again?"

"Again?"

"Like last week."

I'm looking at her in confusion.

Did we do that when we—when I was a kid?

"I thought you liked it?" she says, pouting.

There's no way I'm going to kiss a little girl. This is way too creepy.

"It was nice, but, you know, I don't think I need to do that anymore. I've had enough practice for now. ... Can't you practice with some of our other friends?"

"Lisa is the only one who wants to kiss me, but she's got braces." She wrinkles her nose in distaste.

I'm sure I'll go nuts if I have to spend the next ten years with Pam and Lisa. ... I could be like a mother to them, I suppose, but they aren't going to enjoy that. I need to find the right level of friendliness and support.

"Pam, you're a beautiful and intelligent girl. You don't have to worry about boys liking you. They will. Trust me. You don't need to practice being a great kisser. You can just be yourself and, if you like the boy, the kisses will be special for you and for him."

She smiled.

There—that didn't sound too much like an adult talking to her. Why do girls put such pressure on themselves? Do boys talk among themselves, wondering if they can kiss well enough to please the girls? ... I doubt it. ... I'm sure they're not practicing on each other, except for the few who will eventually decide that girls weren't the object of their passion.

* * *

It's an afternoon in mid-July. I'm lying on my bed,

reading. Lauren is on her tummy in the middle of the floor playing with a wooden doll house that Dad gave her last Christmas. She's rearranging the furniture and the tiny people while she tells me the story of their day.

The summer is passing in slow motion. I'm spending each morning cleaning and taking care of Lauren. Most afternoons are spent with the young girls in the neighborhood, mostly talking about music and boys. I'm bored, bored, bored.

I've got to find a hobby. This new time branch can't be only about Lauren and Mom; I need to improve my life too. I don't want to wind up with cancer in forty years—like last time.

What about music? I've always envied people who can play a guitar and get a room full of people singing, or simply play by themselves to pass the time, adding a bit of atmosphere to a quiet house.

What am I saying? If there's one thing I learned in fifty-five years is that I have no aptitude for music. I have no sense of pitch, or rhythm, or any of that other stuff that musicians have that I don't even know the names for.

Then there's art. I like art. Not much of an icebreaker at a party, but certainly something to pass the time. I hope I have some creativity, a little sense of beauty.

"I'm going to the kitchen for a while. Do you want anything?"

Lauren looks up at me over the roof of the doll house, "No, thank you."

In the kitchen I grab the yellow pages and flip to the Associations page where the Boys and Girls Clubs are listed. I call. Yes, the woman says, they have an art program. I have to fill out an application. Dues are ten dollars per year, but there's some funding if my parents can't afford it.

Great.

* * *

One week later, I'm registered for the summer art program from two to four o'clock each Tuesday and Thursday.

Six girls and two boys are scattered between two tables. The instructor is Mrs. Schmitt, a stern, elderly woman who retired from teaching art at a Catholic high school. She explains that we'll start by exploring drawing, sculpture and ceramics, then after that we can focus on any of the three we want.

By mid-August I'm enthralled with throwing clay on a potter's wheel, making it into cute bowls or coffee mugs. It gives me a chance to get really dirty—clay in my hair, smudges of glaze on my cheeks. Mrs. Schmitt is teaching me how to create glazes of different colors, and how to trim the bottom of a pot so it has a rounded bottom and a foot. Creative juices are flowing. Time is passing more quickly.

Chapter 8

THE SUMMER OF 1967 is over. I'm starting the fourth grade.

As George Costanza will say in a "Seinfeld" episode, about twenty-five years from now, "Kill me, Jerry. Kill me now."

Beyond repeating puberty and menopause, I get to sit through nine years of school again. I should get some kind of award for this!

Oh well ... I was a dull, average student the first time around; I'll try to learn something useful this time. I might absorb some English grammar; I don't remember any of it at the moment, beyond verbs and nouns. I seem to know how to put a sentence together, but can't tell you why I write something one way, but not another.

I was weakest in geography, couldn't locate most countries on a map—still can't. And math! Yikes! This time—thank God!—as I struggle through algebra and trig, I'll be more relaxed, knowing that I will never, ever, put them to any use what-soever.

My teacher is Miss Murphy, a chubby woman about twenty-five who could be my daughter. She says I'm precocious. I'm sure no teacher called me that the first time I was in elementary school. I never really cared for school, certainly not enough to be precocious.

I remember that when I was ten, time seemed to pass at a glacial pace. A day could be an eternity. Well, they are even slower the second time. There aren't words to describe how dull these school days are. And I thought I was bored during the summer!

Mom's divorce was final two weeks ago. She's doing well. With each passing week, she seems less affected by Dad's leaving. Mom is finding a few girlfriends; she has more now than before Dad left.

Mom has full custody of Lauren and me. In the divorce agreement, we're to spend one weekend a month with Dad. We'll see how that goes; I'm not too excited about spending time with him and Cynthia, his new woman. I guess it would be OK if Dad was by himself.

A month ago Lauren stopped sleeping in my bed every night. Lately she only joins me when she has nightmares which isn't often. Sometimes in the early evening, when I'm lying in bed reading, she'll bring one of her stuffed animals so the three of us can cuddle for ten minutes or so—just to be close—then she'll run off and play by herself. It's so easy to adore her now; I'm sure she feels it.

Lauren goes to kindergarten in the morning. She seems outgoing and happy. She comes home most days giggling with stories of her friends at school.

* * *

Friday night.

As she has for the last few weeks, Mom is going out with some single women who are in their late twenties and looking desperately for Mr. Right. Mom is not looking, just having some laughs with women close to her own age. I've been monitoring her progress when she comes home. So far it's only been the women dancing and drinking. When she starts dating, I'll see if I can't go on the date with her.

> *... and treat the man to visions of drowning kittens if he doesn't treat her right! Hee, hee!*

Linda, a friend of mine who lives in our building arrives at eight. Mom has been insisting we have a babysitter so I talked her into letting Linda babysit. Linda is twelve and quite mature for her age.

Mom's girlfriends pull up and honk the horn. Lauren and I get a quick smooch on the cheek, then she's off. I wish I could have connected with her before the date so I could hang out with her. It would be interesting to see her emotions while she's out having fun.

Linda, Lauren and I settle on the couch in the family room to watch Star Trek while we wait for Lauren to get sleepy. Luckily the episode is boring, something about Vulcan biology and betrothal customs, so Lauren is asleep by eight-thirty. Linda carries her into our room and tucks her in.

I pour two Cokes for Linda and myself. I walk over to the TV to turn the volume down.

When are they going to invent TV remotes?

"How do you feel about the war?" asks Linda, re-entering the room.

> *Which war? Oh! Vietnam. Right!*

After a thoughtful pause, I tell her, "I think history will see it as a big mistake."

"Me too. They say it's only partially about fighting communism. It's mostly about oil."

"Everything we do seems to be about oil."

> *Hmm ... Was that a blunder? That might be less true in 1967 than it will be in the next fifty years after the oil crisis of the seventies.*

Linda says, "Most people are saying we shouldn't be there. My Dad says it's their civil war and we should let them fight it—that we're never going to defeat the North Vietnamese."

"I'm sure that's true."

> *I need to change the subject. I don't remember the history of the war; I might talk about something that hasn't happened yet.*

We watch the last few minutes of Star Trek in silence. After that we watch a few minutes of Accidental Family, but get bored and switch to the CBS Friday Night Movies which is half over and not much better. I decide to connect with Linda to see how she feels. I really like her, so it's easy to open a channel.

> *It seems that she's bored too. It's frustrating to be living before cable TV, before DVDs or even VHS tapes— only three channels. She seems to like me, but thinks of me as too young to be her friend. I can feel that she's starting to have sexual fantasies about boys. I'll start a conversation she can relate to.*

"Do you have a boyfriend yet?" I ask.

She hesitates for several seconds. "There's a boy in my class. We like each other, but my parents don't let me date yet."

"Has he kissed you?"

> *Maybe I can seem more mature with this line of questioning. She's taking a while to answer.*

"You won't tell anyone, right?"

"I swear."

"He goes to our school. You met him, Donnie, the blond guy—lives in a house behind these apartments. He's thirteen. We've been alone a few times at school. I thought he was going to kiss me, but in the end I had to kiss him; he seemed like he wanted to kiss me, but was too shy. So I just grabbed him."

"They say that we mature faster than boys."

"We do. He didn't seem to know what to do at all. It was OK though."

"He's really cute. Does he call you?"

"No, we only see each other at school."

"We could go to the shopping center sometime with some of the kids from the neighborhood, including Donnie, and hang out together, get an ice cream or go to a movie. He might not be so shy if there were more people."

"Excellent!"

We watch TV for a while. Linda seems lost in reverie, so I open a channel to her again.

> *So that's it; her mind is racing with fantasies of Donnie in the movie theater. She's quite a little sexpot. That's cute.*

I close the channel and leave her to her thoughts. I wait for her attention to return to the movie, then suggest, "We could organize the kids to go to the movies this Sunday afternoon."

Her eyes light up. "Yes! I'll call some of the girls tomorrow."

At eleven, I say good night and go to my room to dress

for bed. I can hear the clunk-clunk of the channel knob as Linda changes channels looking for something interesting. She's watching *Johnny Carson* when Mom returns at eleven forty-five.

I switch off the light beside my bed when I hear Mom saying good night to Linda, then pretend to be asleep when she sticks her head into our room to check on Lauren and me. Soon I hear her getting ready for bed, rattling around in the bathroom. When her bed springs squeak, I open a channel.

She's relaxed. I wander in her emotions to see if any men were involved in this relaxation, but it seems tonight was another girls' night out—laughter and drinks.

> *Oh! That's interesting. She's considering becoming a realtor. One of the women offered her a job if she can get a realtor's license. Wow! That would be better than cashiering at 7-Eleven when she's forty. I'll send her a big hug and close the channel so I can get some sleep.*

* * *

Saturday morning.

I hear Mom stirring so I go to the kitchen to put the coffee on. After a quick trip to the bathroom, I'm back, making the toast and setting out the butter and jam.

Mom shuffles into the kitchen looking as if she may have had one drink too many last night. I fix her coffee and rub her shoulders while she takes her first sips. Guessing that she would prefer a silent greeting, I reach around and kiss her cheek quietly.

I want to ask her if she's going to get a realtor's license, but can't imagine a way to ask the question without letting her know that I'm reading her emotions and some of her thoughts. I pour myself an orange juice, then munch on a piece of toast while glancing occasionally at Mom's face.

*　*　*

Noon.

We're on our way home from the grocery store. Lauren is excited; she's sitting in the front seat between Mom and me, telling us a long story about a boy at school who wets his pants whenever we say the pledge of allegiance. When she finishes the story she grabs my hand in both of hers and holds it on her lap. Smiling, she looks up at me.

"Mom, have you thought about getting a job? I'd be glad to take care of Lauren if you needed to work."

"Actually, yes, I have thought about it. Tina was telling me that I could work in her realty office if I got a realtor's license."

"I think that would be fantastic!"

"I don't know. Realtors work all kinds of strange hours. I couldn't always be home to fix dinner."

"Mom, I have to grow up sometime; right? I can learn to fix some meals. Lauren and I have a good time together, don't we, Munchkin?"

"Mom! Tell her not to call me Munchkin," says the Munchkin.

"Cailyn! You know she doesn't like that. ... I don't think now is the right time for me to get a job; maybe later. I'll consider getting a realtor's license in a few years. By the time I get one, you'll be a little older, so it might be OK."

*　*　*

The next weekend is our first weekend with Dad and Cynthia. They pick us up on Friday night to take us to a restaurant.

I remember how much I hated Cynthia the first time I lived through 1967. She was an evil witch, or at least, I treated her as one.

Tonight, I want to dislike Cynthia, but I just can't do it. She is being really nice to us.

Was she this nice before? ... It was me, wasn't it?

She's only a few years younger than Mom, so I can't hate her for being a younger bimbo that lured an older man away from his loving wife. She's pretty and seems smart. If I'm going to hate her, I'll have to work at it.

The Italian restaurant is family style, where they bring out big bowls of food and everyone takes their share. Cynthia is friendly and courteous; she makes sure that Lauren and I have what we want. She does this with effortless grace.

I'm watching my emotions as the evening progresses. I suppose the reason this experience is more pleasant—compared to my first trip through 1967—is that it feels as if forty years have passed since Dad left me. I've been over the pain of abandonment for at least thirty years, so Dad and Cynthia seem more like younger friends of mine rather than my Dad and his home-wrecker girlfriend. The person I relate to as my Dad is the old guy who came to visit me in 2012, right after my fall. He only came once, but I didn't really want him to come more often; there's not much to do when a person is in a coma.

Lauren is being shy around Cynthia. Even though she's confused that her father is with this strange woman, I can tell that she likes Cynthia; she smiles whenever Cynthia talks to her.

*   *   *

Saturday is more of the same with Cynthia being infuriatingly pleasant. Hour after hour I expect her to be spoiled and demanding, but she remains stubbornly selfless. A small part of me insists that she's faking it, but the rest knows she isn't. I'm being careful to keep my facial expressions pleasant so I don't influence Lauren the wrong way.

We go to the zoo in the afternoon. Cynthia is very attentive, frequently asking what we want to see next, making sure we have a good time. Both Dad and Cynthia are making a good impression.

That night, while Dad plays a card game with Lauren in the living room, Cynthia and I prepare pork chops for dinner. We find that we work together well.

"I'm really surprised that you know your way around a kitchen," she says.

I look up from slicing carrots, "I try to take some of the load off my mother."

"That's kind of you, but not too many girls know how to use a knife so well."

I smile.

I am precocious after all.

*   *   *

Saturday night, after everyone is in bed, I decide to connect with Cynthia and Dad.

I connect with Cynthia first. She's asleep. I'm glad they're not having sex; that would be disturbing.

I'm wandering in her emotions, still looking for an excuse to dislike her, but she isn't cooperating. She is obviously kind; she likes us; she loves Dad. She seems a genuinely good person.

Damn!

I connect with Dad. He is content with her, but his head is full of his hardware store problems, even in his sleep.

His emotions seem centered on the store. How does he do that? Is he dreaming of hammers and nails? Here he is with a sweet, pretty woman and he's dreaming of his inventory.

I started this weekend believing that she wasn't good enough for him. Now I think it's probably the other way around.

Enough of this—I'll break the connection.

They take us home early Sunday afternoon. As we stand next to the car in the driveway, I stretch up to kiss Cynthia on the cheek and tell her I'm glad she is taking such good care of my Dad. There is a moment after that kiss during which she looks deep into my eyes; I get the feeling that she can sense that I am not really a ten-year-old girl. Thankfully, I don't think she believes what she feels.

When I walk into the kitchen, Mom is washing dishes and looking out the window over the sink, watching Dad drive away. I put my arms around her waist, then lay my head on her upper back.

That night in my diary I write:

2 October 1967

Mother stands at the sink,
staring through the window,
drying a dish;
her hands frozen,
gazing at a past vanished,
the wishes filled with wonders;
she asks where it all went
so quickly
so quickly.

Chapter 9

We moved to the apartment a few weeks ago, so Dad could sell the house. I'm stretched out on the living room floor reading *A Wrinkle in Time* by Madeleine L'Engle, a great book about travel in time and space. Compared to when I read the book decades ago, I am finding that I can completely relate to Meg, the fourteen-year-old heroine.

"I think TM would be so good for you," says Denise, talking to Mom in the kitchen, "and maybe Cailyn too."

I stop to listen to their conversation. Denise is one of Mom's younger friends, a bit of a hippy. Her apartment is in the building next to ours.

"I've been considering it," says Mom. "I first heard about transcendental meditation about a month ago. My sister, Evelyn, and her boyfriend, started doing it. She recommends it too. But I don't know about Cailyn. Do they instruct children?"

"There's several children who come to the center. They even have simplified meditations for preschool children."

"How do they get them to sit still?"

"The length of the meditation depends on the child's age. For the youngest children, they use a walking meditation of just a few minutes."

"So what does it cost?"

"The guy who taught me, Gerard, charges only seventy-five bucks, and it's really easy to learn."

"What has it done for you so far?"

"I think it's mostly about being calm, but Gerard says that eventually you see your life more clearly. You know yourself better and make better choices—something like that."

"I could certainly use more clarity."

"The Beatles are doing it. Did you hear that they all went to India earlier this year to spend time with the maharishi?"

"Evelyn was telling me about that. She also said that the maharishi tried to rape Mia Farrow while she was in India with the Beatles."

"Well, he may be a dirty old man, but the meditation still works."

"Give me Gerard's number and I'll give him a call."

*　*　*

The following Saturday afternoon, Mom and I walk through the front door of a small storefront on Euclid Avenue that is being used as a meditation center. Gerard greets us with a smile. He seems as if he's a really nice guy—pleasantly mellow. We give him our gifts, two small bunches of flowers that represent an offering to the teacher.

He takes us into a small room that has three chairs

along one wall. On an altar against the opposite wall are candles, incense, and other gifts—some fruit and more flowers. He does a short ceremony with the stuff on the altar.

He explains the basic process of repeating a mantra for twenty minutes, then he whispers my mother's mantra to her. She sits and starts to meditate.

He whispers mine in my ear.

"How do you spell that?" I ask; I have no idea what he said.

"I can't spell it for you; just listen carefully."

He says it again.

"It sounds like you're saying "shrink.""

"Almost. Don't say it out loud. Listen again."

He repeats the mantra three times.

"OK. I think I have it now."

He tells me to sit in one of the chairs then repeat the mantra slowly until he tells me to stop.

> *shring ... shring ... shring ...*

> *There's something to this. I can feel myself relaxing a little. ... shring ... shring ... Where are all these thoughts coming from? I'm not supposed to be having thoughts, dammit. ...*

> *shring ... shring ... shring ...*

> *This isn't working for me; I'm only wallowing in my stuff. ...*

> *shring ... shring ... shring ... shring ...*

I'll open a channel to Gerard to see what's going on with him. ...

Ah ha! It seems that he's wallowing too. Some of his thoughts involve checking Mom out. Interesting. At least he isn't checking me out! ...

shring ... shring ... shring ...

"It's been twenty minutes," says Gerard quietly. "Don't open your eyes yet. Just take two minutes to return to normal consciousness."

I am at normal consciousness.

"Stop the mantra and just relax. Take a few breaths."

That was interesting. I'll have to do it at home and be more serious.

After our eyes are open, Gerard gives us more instructions. At the end he says, "We have a session for new meditators every Friday evening at seven-thirty. We find it helps to meditate as a group then talk about experiences, answer questions, whatever."

"Great!" says Mom. "We'll see you on Friday."

* * *

The next Friday we're walking out of the group session when one of the other women stops us.

"Excuse me. Lottie, is it?"

"Yes."

"Hi. I'm Helen Radnitz. I'm wondering if you and your daughter want to go have a coffee or soda. I really connected with the questions you were asking. I thought we should get to know each other."

Mom looks at me. I smile.

"Sure," Mom says. "There's a café about four doors down. Why don't we go there? I don't want to be out too late. My younger daughter is at home with a sitter."

The café is run down and devoid of customers, but clean. A smiling round woman in her fifties, waves for us to sit anywhere. We slide into a booth at the front.

She walks over. "I'm Mrs. Mitzotakis. What can I bring you to drink?"

A man in an apron sits at a back table listening and watching with a completely bland expression over the top of a Greek newspaper. I assume he is the husband and the cook. Since we're only having drinks, without moving a single facial muscle, he returns to his paper.

"I moved here from Denver two years ago," says Helen, "when my husband got transferred. So the jerk gets involved with another woman, a skinny little bitch—sorry—almost immediately. So I divorced him ten months ago."

The owner brings coffees for Mom and Helen, a milk for me.

"Well, we have that in common," says Mom, "except I've always lived here."

"I've had a tough time meeting people my age," says Helen. "I'm not into bars. I thought if I joined TM, I'd meet some people who were interested in a healthy lifestyle."

"I don't know how healthy we are, but we try. ... Do you have children?"

"No. We weren't married very long."

"Where do you work?"

"I've started a New Age shop. It's on Superior Avenue a bit farther out. I sell books, crystals, incense, candles and jewelry. You should drop in some time."

"I will. It sounds interesting. ... I'm not working yet," says Mom. "I might go to work after the girls get a little older."

The owner brings over two small cookies on a plate. "May I offer these to your daughter?"

I smile. Mom smiles. I thank her. She returns to sit with her husband.

There are still no other customers. I'm concerned that we may be keeping the owners from closing, but Mom and Helen are oblivious; they chat for another half hour, exchange phone numbers, then we leave.

Over the next six weeks we visit the café every Friday after the meditation. The cookies become a weekly treat, because, Mrs. Mitzotakis tells me on the second visit, she misses her granddaughter who lives in New York. It seems she looks a little like me.

After the first visit, Mr. Mitzotakis stopped listening for food orders. Some nights he would stay hidden behind the paper. On other nights he would start cleaning the kitchen.

On the first Saturday in October, Mom, Lauren and I drive up Superior Avenue to visit Helen's shop, *The Crystal Cottage*. We enter a street door with a large glass panel covered with bumper stickers that urge "Make Love Not War," "Humphrey-Muskie 1968," and "Dare to be Naive." The wooden parts of the door look as if they've been painted a dozen times by people who were less than professional painters.

Helen has created a place of wonder, colorfully decorated and full of intriguing items.

There are three customers as we arrive, hippies buying incense and books. We look around while she rings up their purchases. Mom and I browse the book section while Lauren uses a finger to delicately spin the crystals catching the sunlight that fills the front window display.

I find a copy of Maharishi's translation of the *Bhagavad Gita*. Mom glances through an illustrated volume of Rumi's poetry.

We move to the conversation nook that Helen has created in a rear corner of the shop. Lauren joins us, settling into a beanbag chair with a book on fairies while Helen goes in the back to fetch a juice for Lauren and two cups of herb tea for Mom and me. We sink into overstuffed chairs then talk mostly about our meditation experiences. Eventually there's a lull while the three of us sip our tea.

"You know," says Helen, "I could really use some help if you wanted a job. You could bring the girls to work with you."

"Do you really have that many customers?" asks Mom.

"It's not that, although I'm doing pretty well. The problem is I'm always by myself so if I need to run an errand, I have to close the shop. And sometimes two or three people will come in at once and I don't feel I have enough time to spend with each one."

"What hours would you want me to work?

"Could you do one to six, Monday through Saturday?"

"We'll talk it over and call you early next week. I'd like to, if we can work out a way to take care of the girls' needs."

Both Lauren and I like the shop and want Mom to work there. That evening, we work out our schedule. Through the week, after school, Lauren and I will go to another apartment in our building where a retired lady lives with her two cats. On Saturday we'll go to work with Mom.

*   *   *

The following Saturday, we drive up Superior for our first day of work. Helen shows us around the shop. It's almost like a toy shop; there are kaleidoscopes and Buddhist singing bowls to play with, crystals in the front window to spin and watch the rainbows flash along the walls. The rear third of the store is for storage. Here, Helen has arranged a table and chairs as a play or study area for Lauren and me. There's a toilet and a small kitchenette. The smell from the boxes of incense and candles is almost overpowering.

*   *   *

Late November.

It's Saturday afternoon at *The Crystal Cottage*. Lauren and I are in the back room. Lauren is reading while I unpack some new supplies that the mailman delivered today. I'm putting packages of incense on the shelves while eavesdropping on Helen's conversation with a customer through the paisley curtain separating us from the customer area.

"You must come, Helen," says the customer whose voice I don't recognize, "He's really a fascinating swami."

"That sounds great. What time shall we come? Lottie

can come too, right?"

"Of course, there's plenty of room. Come at eight."

"Can I bring my two daughters?" Mom asks, "My eleven-year-old is a meditator and I can bring some books to keep the six-year-old busy."

"Swamiji loves children. I'm sure we can keep the little one happy while we meditate."

*   *   *

At eight, the four of us are standing outside a large house in Shaker Heights. The gray stone walls and heavy wooden door give the impression of an English castle—well, perhaps the back door of one.

The door opens to a smiling face, "Welcome, I'm Irene."

We all introduce ourselves.

"Follow me to the yoga studio," says Irene.

With the faint smell of incense getting stronger, we follow her down quite a long hall to a room that once might have been a glassed-in patio. The room is subtly lighted with concealed lighting around the upper edges of the walls, and carpeted with a padded berber that makes a wall-to-wall yoga mat. The swami is in the far corner, seated in the full lotus position on a low meditation seat made of wicker with a high rounded back. The others, about fifteen, some of whom I recognize from Helen's store, are seated in rough semicircles around the swami.

I expected to see an old man like the pictures of the maharishi, but this swami is completely different. Wearing a plum-colored robe, he is beautiful, clean-shaven and younger than I expected. He's forty-ish and very dark complected. As we walk in and settle ourselves at the back of the small crowd, he is giggling at something said by one of those standing near him. Irene offers us some cushions. There are no chairs in the room other than the seat the swami is sitting on.

The swami catches my eye, smiles, then motions for me to come to him. While I begin walking toward him, he motions for Lauren to come too. As we approach, he smiles beautifully with incredibly white teeth. He takes two red roses from a bouquet at his side, then hands one to each of us. He puts his hands in a prayerful position and bows to us. I feel excused, so I take Lauren's hand to return to our seats.

Irene says, "We're going to meditate with Swamiji for about twenty minutes. I hope everyone understands that he does not speak. Being silent is part of his practice. He hasn't spoken since taking a vow of silence many years ago. You might find that he speaks to your heart in other ways."

Mom settles Lauren with several books to read in a far corner of the room. I hear her repeat her instructions to be silent until the meditation is finished. Over the last few months that Mom and I have been meditating, Lauren has become used to respecting our meditation time. Sometimes she sits with us with her eyes closed for a few minutes, then quietly goes to her room to play.

We all start with pranayama, a yoga breathing exercise that calms the mind, then drift into meditation. I can sense the meditators around me, much as in the group meditations at the TM center, but tonight is a bit more mellow. I wonder if the swami is having an effect on us.

After a few minutes of mantra meditation, some worries wandered into my mind. Once I was aware that I had stopped the mantra, I decided it would be interesting to open a channel to the swami since I may never have another chance to wander in a swami's thoughts and feelings. The channel opens easily.

Wow! This guy is really blissful. Most people are a jumble of thoughts and feelings, but he is ... how can I describe it? It's like ...

Swamiji: Welcome, my dear.

Uhh. ... O my God! Hi. ... I didn't know you could tell I was connected.

Swamiji: Yes, I felt something about you when you walked into the room.

How are you able to talk to me like this?

Swamiji: My dear. I should ask you—how are you able to talk to me?

(He's laughing.)

I have been able to sense other people's feelings for some time, Swamiji, but this is the first time I've been able to talk to someone through the connection. Can you explain what's happening?

Swamiji: Yes, Dear. ... The mind has several parts. At present my buddhi is talking to your buddhi. The buddhi is your spiritual mind that watches the other parts. The buddhi is related to your conscience, but it is much more than that. When you are connected to most people, your buddhi is connected to their chitta, our Sanskrit word for their lasting impressions from their life so far. You can think of chitta as memories.

Thank you. ... Sometimes I'm able to make people feel or see something. What is going on then?

Swamiji: When you give someone else a smell,

or vision, or any other feeling, your buddhi is speaking to the part of their mind that we call manas in India. This part of their mind is the interface with the physical world, the senses and their current actions. I hope you will use this carefully; it can cause problems if you make people see or hear things that are not there. They might worry they are going insane.

Yes, I'll be careful.

Swamiji: I notice that you are an old woman in this young girl's body. You have come back in time. ... I see you've come to help your sister and your mother.

Yes. No one else knows that. Please keep my secret.

Swamiji: It is best kept a secret. And I hope you will not tell anyone that I am a chatterbox!

(Swamiji is giggling.)

I will keep your secret too. ... Can I talk to you again if I need to?

Swamiji: Yes, my dear. Even when I am in India, you can talk to me anytime. I am here to help, but now let us go back to the meditation so I can concentrate on these delightful people.

I feel our connection close, then I seem to be floating in the blackness of outer space. I watch my breath for a few moments before restarting my mantra, but the sound of it is very faint as if it is under water. There is what seems only a few seconds of bliss before a tiny bell sounds a single "ting" to indicate the end of the meditation. Those "few seconds" must have been ten minutes.

The bliss continues after the meditation. A few more minutes of breath work, then I open my eyes to find

Swamiji looking at me. I bow slightly and send the thought of "namaste" to him. He giggles out loud.

I love this guy.

No one seems to want to move. A few of the more flexible people stretch forward to rest their upper bodies on their legs. Others lie on their backs. After about five minutes, Irene and a few others start to move about. We hear the sounds of plates and silverware in an adjoining room.

More people start to move around. A few people leave the room to collect their tea and hors d'oerves while others take turns sitting at Swamiji's feet, assuming, I suppose, that nearness to him creates some special blessing. Those not sitting near him are in small groups talking quietly, sipping tea and nibbling. I sit across the room from him, using the wall as a backrest. The thought crosses my mind that proximity to him is irrelevant. He glances at me and giggles. I smile back at him and bow slightly in his direction.

Mom gives Lauren a glass of juice and a napkin with two cookies. She eats the cookies immediately, then, juice in hand, wanders among the adults, looking up at the faces. Once she reaches the other side of the room, she edges along the wall, moving closer and closer to the swami. She sits down to his left with her back to the wall, so she is slightly behind him and hidden from his view by the tall back of the seat. I catch glimpses of her sipping her juice in the gaps between the adults who are gathered near the swami. There is a small table on Swamiji's right. Irene places a plate of cookies and a cup of tea on the table. While Swamiji continues to smile and nod at the adults around him, he takes one of his cookies and passes it around the left edge of the seat. I can't see Lauren, but I see him bring his hand back without the cookie.

I really love this guy.

Chapter 10

"Cailyn, please hurry," Mom calls from the open kitchen door, "I want to get on the road."

I'm lugging my suitcase down the linoleum hallway toward the kitchen. I can barely lift it with these little-girl arms. Lauren is trying to follow with hers, but she can't budge it. She's tugging at the handle and making straining noises. Mom comes to help her.

Mom hoists the bags into the trunk of her big '65 Plymouth, then we head east for a six-hour drive. Mom's younger sister Evelyn, in Rochester, New York, has been begging her to come visit ever since the divorce.

The drive on the parkway is hot and boring. We're driving parallel to the shore of Lake Erie, but the road is too far from the lake to see anything but farms and trees. There's no air conditioning; we've cracked the rear windows and opened the front vent windows to keep the air moving through the car. My bare legs are sticking to the plastic seats and making sucking sounds whenever I move them.

Laura is lying on the back seat reading. I'm sitting in the front with Mom, hoping to be entertaining. I really can't get into the license plate game or "I spy" that might have kept us busy when I was twelve the first time.

"Tell me more about Aunt Evelyn," I say, "I don't think I remember her well."

Actually I remember Evelyn very well, but as she was in the eighties and nineties when she was in marketing for Kodak. I can't picture her in the sixties.

"I think you'll like her; she's a bit of an artist—at least she believes she is. ... She does watercolors and jewelry."

"Is she married?"

"No, she's living with a guy."

"Does she make a living with art, or does she have to do something else?"

"Oh, I think she works at an office somewhere, and takes courses at the Rochester Institute of Technology."

I stare at the fields flying by on the right for a few miles.

"How long are we going to stay?"

"Perhaps a few weeks. We don't need to return until you're ready to start school."

"What are we going to do for two weeks?" I couldn't help letting concern creep into my voice.

"We'll have a good time. Evelyn will take us to see all the artsy shops and museums. We can go see Niagara Falls; you've never seen it."

I have seen the falls—twice in the 1980s, but that was in my pre-coma life. I'm looking forward to seeing them again.

We arrive in Rochester about six.

Evelyn greets us at the door to her apartment, wearing a headband with a native American motif, a tie-dyed dress that fits her like a tent, sandals and no bra. Her boyfriend, Morris, is straightening up the living room which matches Evelyn's outfit.

Morris is hairy; he looks as if he could be a poster child for the sixties—beard, moustache and a pony-tail reaching the bottom of his shoulder blades. He seems like a decent guy, full of smiles as he tries to entertain Lauren and me with some excellent guitar-playing while Mom and Evelyn are making the dinner, laughing as they catch up on their lives.

In my pre-coma life, I was never intimate with a hairy guy. While Morris sings I keep looking at his mouth, how the hairs of his moustache hang straight down, past his lower lip. As I imagine Evelyn kissing him, I have a vision of a woman walking through a field of waist-high grass, pushing the stalks out of the way to form a path. I imagine kissing Wilford Brimley, the old guy in the oatmeal commercials, then, for a moment, my mind wanders to kissing Tom Selleck on Magnum P.I., but that's too distracting. Of course, Morris's moustache and beard might give a girl a tickle if he was kissing the right body parts.

I should pay more attention to the music.

After dinner we sit, talking about the war and the escalating conflicts with the protesters. Evelyn and Morris are much more aware of the politics that are behind both sides. Mom and I haven't been following the war or the protest movement, so we mostly nod and smile while Evelyn and Morris talk.

After dinner, Lauren is bored. I offer to help her get ready for bed so Mom and Evelyn can continue to talk; they're obviously really enjoying each other.

Evelyn takes us upstairs to show us our room and where to wash up.

Lauren and I shower, dress for bed, then lay down to read some of the books that Lauren brought with her. It's almost midnight when Mom joins us. She moves Lauren to a loveseat that is just big enough for her to sleep on. I'm glad that I get to sleep with Mom. It's been many years since I did. She turns her back to me. I press up against her with my arm around her waist. She smells of roses from the perfumed soap.

I open a channel to check on her. She's elated. I sense her deep relationship with Evelyn which reminds me of my love for Lauren. I'm too tired to wander in her emotions. I fall asleep while we're still connected.

* * *

The next day Morris shows us an ad in one of the New York papers for the "Woodstock Music and Arts Fair" coming up the next weekend in White Lake. Morris thinks it will be groovy. I have to laugh to myself, knowing what I know, while Mom and Evelyn argue with him that it's not worth it to drive half-way across the state with two kids.

I take Morris's side and plead that I'll help take care of Lauren. Morris keeps repeating the long list of famous bands that will be there. He and I prevail. I really don't want to miss Woodstock twice in one lifetime.

* * *

Getting to the concert the following Friday is long and miserable. The line of cars is forever. We're in Morris's VW Beetle; no air conditioning, August, no breeze—you get the picture. The roads, as we get closer, can't handle the traffic. Several times Mom says she wants to turn around and return to Rochester, but Morris is insistent.

It takes eight hours from the time we reached the end of the line of cars until we find a place to park that is close enough that we can walk the rest of the way. Mom and Morris take turns carrying sweaty Lauren who fell asleep in the car. A few minutes before ten, we arrive, exhausted and hungry, at Max Yasgur's farm after walking two miles from where we parked.

We expect to buy tickets at the gate, but by the time we get there, the crowd has pushed down the perimeter fence on West Shore Road, so everyone is simply walking in. We walk down Hurd Road until we get to the top of the slope that forms the seating area, then we wind our way through a sea of two hundred thousand people.

As we proceed down the hill toward the stage, there is no music. A guy at the microphone is making announcements. We're walking through a dense haze of marijuana smoke.

As we settle onto a vacant patch of Mr. Yasgur's freshly mowed pasture, Ravi Shankar begins playing. It starts raining immediately, but Shankar manages to play three songs. We brought five big umbrellas, so we sit huddled together so the umbrellas combine to form a canopy over us. Morris and Mom sit toward the rear of the blanket. I use Mom for a backrest. Evelyn cuddles up against Morris's chest. Lauren sleeps in the middle, wrapped in a second blanket. As Ravi Shankar plays, Morris keeps oo-ing and ah-ing. Never having heard Indian music before, he's really interested in what the sitar master is doing.

The sound is great. We're about two hundred feet from the stage so the volume is loud, but not painful.

There's constant movement around us; people pouring in, moving closer to the stage. The influx continues all night.

Melanie Safka plays for a half hour after Shankar finishes—soft folksy ballads in her husky voice. I had forgotten her long ago. After a twenty minute break with a lot of equipment movement on stage, Arlo Guthrie sings a bunch of drug-related songs that I don't remember hearing during the sixties, and can't relate to. I was probably too young for his stuff during my original life, and too old for it now.

I want to stay up to see Joan Baez; I always respected her and what she stood for. I'm fighting sleep throughout the half-hour break while they setup the stage for her. It's one in the morning when she comes out to sing *O Happy Day*. The day, or at least the night, would be a bit happier if I could have slept a few hours before she started singing. Next she sings, *The Last Thing on My Mind*—and it was; I sleep through the other songs of her set and wake up to daylight and the sound of voices all around me.

I'm frightened. Helicopters are flying overhead. Trucks and tractors with loud diesel engines are moving along the edges of the crowd. It seems as if there's some kind of emergency, but no one else is excited.

"What's going on?" I ask.

"Don't know," says Evelyn, "just getting set up, I guess."

Evelyn is pulling breakfast out of a small cooler she brought. The rain has stopped. Evelyn hands me a sandwich and a bottle of grape juice. Lauren is sitting on the blanket at our feet eating her sandwich.

"Where's Morris?" I ask.

"He went up there somewhere (she points up the hill to our left) to find out where everything is," says Evelyn. "It was too dark when we got here last night."

I stand up and look around. I can see people at the top of the hill setting up big tents. Later I would learn these were the first aid stations and some of the food facilities.

"Can we go somewhere?" I ask.

"Where do you want to go?" asks Mom.

"I don't know. Anywhere, I guess."

"I can stay here and watch our stuff if you want to walk around with the girls," says Evelyn.

"Maybe we should move around a bit," answers Mom. Then to Evelyn she says, "We'll be back when the music starts, or maybe before then."

We walk to the top of the hill, so we can visit a long row of portable toilets. We have to stand in line for a longer time than is comfortable. We all really need to pee. That need satisfied, we continue walking around the concession area to see what's going on. It's a flurry of activity; people are working to expand the facilities to match the size of the crowd. Next to the concessions is a playground, so we let Lauren play on a swing for a few minutes.

"Can we go check out the stage area?" I ask while I push Lauren's swing. "We might see someone famous."

Mom smiles.

We slip through the crowds toward the seating area, then along the edge of the audience to the stage. The field is getting really muddy from all the people milling around in the rain-soaked grass.

We reach the fence that's protecting the stage area. I hoped there would be a famous band setting up, but it's only a local group, called *Quill*, getting their equipment arranged and connected. When we tire of standing there watching guitars and keyboards being plugged into amplifiers, we return to our blanket.

The music starts again at noon; Quill is followed by another rock band that I've never heard of. At two o'clock, the soon-to-be-famous Santana comes on stage. This is the concert that makes him a legend. It is fun listening to the reactions of the audience near us who have never heard of him. His Latin-rock style is so different from the other groups playing this weekend. The crowd is literally jumping up and down, singing *Oye como va, mi ritmo*, getting into the "ritmo" of his music. I feel the ground shaking a little.

> *I don't know why I'm crying. Maybe I'm just so grateful to be here to listen to this moment in history.*

Other than the hour of listening to Santana, Lauren and I are bored through the daylight hours. She's getting a bit whiny. Even with my fifty-five-year-old mind, or perhaps because of it, there's only so much sixties rock and roll a girl can take—unless she's stoned which I'm not. Although all of us are probably somewhat high from the constant marijuana fog.

Mom had laid down the law to Evelyn and Morris: there were to be no drugs during the weekend. I suspect Morris had a few tokes as he wandered around without us.

By late afternoon on Saturday, we are all starving. We'd only brought enough food for breakfast and lunch. We thought we could buy food when that ran out, and we could have, if a hundred thousand people had shown up instead of over four hundred thousand. The organizers are having trouble bringing in the food fast enough.

As Morris, Evelyn and Mom are discussing the situation, someone on the stage announces that the wonderful people of Bethel, New York, have made sandwiches—thousands of them—for the concert. The adults leave to get in line while Lauren and I sit on the blanket, listening to the music—some guys called *The Keef Hartley Band*. They are probably just the thing for the stoners nearby, but not for us. Lauren falls asleep. I wish I could. I lie down with her, but the music is too loud to really sleep.

The adults return after an hour with plates of food—sandwiches and some healthy-looking stew.

After the sun goes down, Lauren and I are even more bored. During the day we can watch the eccentrics in the nearby audience, but now it's too dark, so Lauren and I sit on the blanket while adults, including our three, jump up and down all around us.

The marijuana haze is much stronger. I'm feeling a little buzz. In quiet moments between songs, I can hear a few couples having enthusiastic sex nearby. Mom keeps looking at me, then in the direction of the cries of sexual ecstasy, then back to me. I smile at her and shrug my shoulders. I know she worries I'm being corrupted by all the sex and drugs. I wish there was a way to tell her it was OK.

When I wake up around five o'clock on Sunday morning, Saturday night is still going on. Mom tells me I slept through *The Grateful Dead, Creedence Clearwater Revival,* and *Janis Joplin* who were all supposed to play Saturday evening, but had to play in the early morning hours of Sunday because of all the rain delays.

Mom, Morris and Evelyn all look like ... you know, I'm not sure there's a word for people who are that tired and frazzled from listening to rock music in a muddy pasture for thirty-six hours. The words that first to come to mind aren't descriptive enough. If there was a word that meant totally exhausted while, at the same time, extremely over-stimulated, then that would be the word to use.

The Who play two dozen songs in an hour as the sky is starting to lighten. They get some, but not all, of the people on their feet again. There is a miserable hour break for rain, then *Jefferson Airplane* comes on and plays a dozen wake-you-up songs until almost ten.

Things quiet down for a few hours while the crowd gets some rest. A lot of people, the ones smarter than us, brought tents which they pitched in the woods west of the concession stands. We, due to our gross lack of preparation, take turns lying on our wet blanket, three at a time. During one of the periods when Morris isn't sleeping, he walks up the hill and brings us some breakfast. I love Morris.

The sun comes out. We hear that people are swimming in a lake north of the stage. Since we all need a bath, Mom, Lauren and I walk to the lake while Evelyn and Morris watch our stuff.

I suppose that Mom might have thought that somehow we could bathe in private, but now, as we're standing at the edge of the rapidly expanding crowd who are removing their clothes, it's clear this will be a skinny dip. Poor Mom—here she is with two young daughters and naked adult men are all around us. It takes her a minute before she shrugs her shoulders and looks at me with an "I don't know what to do" look.

"It's OK, Mom," I tell her, "We don't have to look."

But Lauren is looking ... and pointing. We strip off and, holding hands and our clothes, wade into the lake. The bottom is muddy and squishy.

This isn't as bad as I thought it would be. At least a hundred kids are in the water, washing and playing. Everyone is behaving themselves. I walk in until the water is up to my shoulders. Mom is carrying Lauren on her hip. She walks out farther until her boobs are under water. I'm pretty sure exposing herself to dozens of young men is a new experience for her. For me too, now that I think about it, but being in a twelve-year-old body helps; there are plenty of twenty-year-old girls to attract the attention of the twenty-year-old guys. When a guy looks my way, it is only long enough to notice that I'm boobless.

I dip under the water to get my hair wet. It got so tangled while I was sleeping on the ground. When a blond woman nearby sees me struggling to get the muddy tangles out of my hair, she hands me a bottle of shampoo. I take a dollop, then give some to Mom and Lauren. We rinse out our clothes and wring the water from them as best we can. Mom says that we can wear our wet panties and T-shirts until the other clothes dry. At first it seems strange to walk through the crowds in our underwear, but there's so much nudity that we almost seem overdressed.

We rejoin Evelyn and Morris briefly, then they head for the lake while we lay on the blanket. There's no music, so we take a quick nap.

An hour later, Morris and Evelyn return and wake us up. They need to rest so we stand up to give them room to lie down.

By now the field is mostly mud. There is trash everywhere. While we wait for the music to start, Lauren is dancing barefoot around our little group splashing in the mud. She cuts her foot on a pop-top from a soda can and starts crying. We rinse off her foot with a bottle of water, but blood is dripping off her toes. With Mom following, Morris carries her to the first aid tent while Evelyn and I lay on the blanket and close our eyes.

They return after an hour with her foot completely bandaged. Mom says she was impressed with the volunteer doctor who cleaned the wound and stitched her foot. Lauren's barefoot days are over for a week or so, until the wound heals. She can't walk in the mud, so someone will have to carry her for the rest of the weekend.

The music starts again at 2 o'clock. Joe Cocker is his rasping, arm-flailing self. *How did that guy ever have a career?* He croaks for an hour and a half, then the rain starts again—really drenching us this time. We cover up with the umbrellas to wait out the thunderstorm. Many people are using the falling rain to shower—especially the young men who aren't wearing shirts. A few men and women strip completely. Others use the mud to get even dirtier, making a mud-slide down the slope.

My whole adult life, I've thought how great it would have been to be part of Woodstock, to have witnessed one of the counter-cultural high points of the sixties. Now here I am at Woodstock, bored, wet and hungry. The music that I really wanted to hear was mostly late at night as I slept. During the day was mostly second-tier bands that I never heard of.

But there was *Santana.* Maybe it was worth the hassle just to experience him and his band yesterday. That was great.

Finally the rain lets up. The tech crew pulls the tarps from the equipment on stage, then *Country Joe and the Fish* scream for two hours. The crowd loves it. It was a bit too "sixties" for me. At eight o'clock, a British blues band called *Ten Years After* plays for an hour. They are very good but a little too slow for Lauren; she falls asleep before the second song is over. I fall asleep after a few more. It was an exhausting day.

Sometime early Monday morning, I hear *Crosby, Stills, Nash & Young* playing *Marrakesh Express*. At first it seems like a dream. I sit up. Yes, they're on the stage. The sky is just starting to lighten in the east. I'm too tired to sit up; I lie down to listen to them, resting my head on Mom's leg, but I fall back to sleep.

> *Damn! Another group I would have liked to have heard.*

At dawn, as soon as there is light enough to see who we are stepping on, we start hiking to our car. Morris carries Lauren. Mom, Evelyn and I carry muddy blankets, umbrellas and the picnic cooler. Most people are leaving. *The Paul Butterfield Blues Band* is playing some old-time blues. They are great, but, by the time we reach the intersection of West Shore Road and Perry Road, we can only hear the boom of their bass.

About a half mile down Perry Road, we find Morris's VW in the field where we rented a parking space from a farmer. As he pulls onto Perry Road, Morris says we only have a quarter tank of gas, so we need to find some. We pass gas station after gas station, but each has signs saying they are out of gas. I can tell Mom is getting nervous. We barely make it, running on fumes, to a gas station in a small town called Callicoon, New York.

We unfold ourselves from the VW bug. While the gas station attendant fills the tank, I look back toward Mr. Yasgur's farm. Santana's "ritmo" still ringing in my ears.

* * *

Safely back at Morris and Evelyn's apartment on

Monday evening, we find out from one of Morris's friends that while we were in our car, crawling towards Rochester in the traffic jam, Jimi Hendrix started his set at nine that morning. So we missed him playing *The Star-Spangled Banner*—yet another of the defining moments of the sixties!

Aargh!

Lauren and I have a snack, a quick bath, then go to bed exhausted. The grownups stay up for a while, drinking wine and reliving the weekend.

The next morning, Lauren and I fix our own breakfast. No one else surfaces until after nine.

Chapter 11

As I sit down to meditate the next morning, I begin the breathing exercises, then the thought of contacting Swamiji pops into my mind.

He said I could talk to him anytime. I think back to the sweetness of the conversations we had in Shaker Heights. I am reliving his giggles when he interrupts me.

> *Swamiji: Namaste, my dear.*

> *Oh! Swamiji! I just had the thought, and there you are. I didn't think it would be that easy.*

> *Swamiji: I was expecting you.*

> *Really? Why were you expecting me?*

> *Swamiji: What kind of swami would I be if I didn't know you were going to call on me?*

> *I giggle. So does he.*

> *Swamiji: You have a question, my dear.*

> *I don't think so. I wanted to send you some love.*

> *Swamiji: No, there is a question. Let us be still for a moment so you can find it.*

I said my mantra for a few minutes. The meditation was so profound, a blissful emptiness. Then there was a thought of Mom and Lauren and the effect I'm having on them.

> *Could this be the question: am I doing the right thing with my mother and sister? Will this turn out all right?*

> *Swamiji: You are doing well for now. Keep meditating and you will know how to change and when to change. Study the Bhagavad Gita so you will understand duty and detachment. In the years to come there will be decisions to make that require detachment.*

We have Maharishi's translation at home.

> *Swamiji: That book only has the first six chapters. Buy a copy of Isherwood's translation; read the first twelve chapters.*

I will.

> *Swamiji: Have you told anyone that I'm a chatterbox?*

I laugh. No, have you told anyone that I'm an old woman?

(He giggles.)

> *Swamiji: You asked if your mother's and sister's lives would turn out all right. You are able to see that for yourself. But remember these futures are not fixed. I believe you will make the right decisions and arrive at a good end, but the decisions will be sometimes difficult for someone who is attached to the material world. You must rise above this. This is the importance of detachment.*

Thank you, Swamiji.

Swamiji: It is a joy to talk to you. Being silent is quite boring. Call me anytime.

What are you doing now?

Swamiji: I am in a lecture hall. Another swami is giving a talk. I am sitting beside him on the dais, smiling and nodding so he thinks that I agree with him. He is actually a fool, but he's doing no harm. Now I should stop talking to you so I can send him a more correct end to his talk. The students will take that away rather than the materialistic and superstitious rubbish that he's been telling them.

Good-bye, Swamiji. Thank you! ...

The connection breaks.

Jesus! What an experience!

I start the mantra and finish my meditation, but I am too agitated to relax into it. I lie down to get more sleep. I wonder about detachment. I've never heard the word used in a spiritual sense.

On Wednesday we visit a huge bookstore in Rochester that has a copy of Christopher Isherwood's translation of the *Bhagavad Gita*. I start reading it as soon as we get in the car.

The whole visit with Evelyn and Morris is relaxed and exciting at the same time. Just as Mom had told us, we visit all the museums and galleries around Rochester. We see Niagara Falls. Morris is great fun. Throughout the remainder of our stay, he tries to teach Lauren and me to play the guitar. He has more success with Lauren.

The Friday before school starts, we return home riding the sticky plastic seats in Mom's Plymouth. This time I read the Gita the whole way, discussing it with Mom to keep her alert.

* * *

Sunday night.

I'm lying on my back in my own bed. Lauren is asleep in hers. Mom is watching TV. I'm thinking that I should take a peek at the next ten or fifteen years to see where we're headed. Swamiji said I could do it. I'm not sure if he meant that I should do it, but he didn't warn me against it. I decide that I'll only check on their happiness; I won't try to see too much of what's going on in their lives.

I make myself comfortable. I open a channel to Lauren. I spend a moment watching her current emotions which are quite peaceful, then I give a gentle push in the time dimension to start moving into the future.

> *... Ahh, so that's what happens. ... Interesting ...*

> *Did you expect me to spoil the rest of the story for you?*

I decide to check out Mom. I don't want to connect with her while she's watching TV, so I sit on my bed meditating until I hear her come out of the bathroom, then I lay down to wait for the creak of her bed-springs.

I connect with her and move through time as I did with Lauren. I feel OK about what I see. I break the connection.

The thought crosses my mind to check on my own future. Will I be dying of cancer in 2018? Swamiji didn't say I could check on my future, so I'm not going to do it. I'm going to assume that I don't die from cancer. But if I don't get cancer it'll be because I'm going to take much better care of myself this time.

What do I do now? I know this could be a successful time branch. I ask myself: will it be successful because of things I do in the future, or is it better to let time flow without messing with it? There might be an answer in the *Gita*. I fall asleep reading it.

* * *

Monday.

School still hasn't started so, after morning chores, I spend the day reading the *Gita*, taking careful notes.

> *Perform every action with your heart fixed on the Supreme Lord. Renounce attachment to the fruits [of your actions]. Be even-tempered in success and failure ...*

> Bhagavad Gita 2:48

Swamiji talked about detachment which seems the same as "renouncing attachment to the fruits." I found a verse that seemed to be talking about attachment.

> *Thinking about sense-objects will attach you to sense objects;*
>
> *Grow attached, and you become addicted;*
>
> *Thwart your addiction, it turns to anger;*
>
> *Be angry, and you confuse your mind;*
>
> *Confuse your mind,*
>
> *   you forget the lesson of experience;*
>
> *Forget experience, you lose discrimination;*

> *Lose discrimination,*
>
>> *and you miss life's only purpose.*
>>
>>> *Bhagavad Gita 2:62*

Got it! — no thinking about sense objects. It all seems to be about acting for the sake of our duty and for the sake of God, then accepting whatever happens without joy or pain.

How is "discrimination" tied to "life's only purpose"? I believe discrimination is knowing right from wrong, recognizing the flow of dharma in our lives.

> *Melted in the flame of My knowledge,*
>
> *Turning his face from the fruit,*
>
> *He needs nothing: The Atman is enough.*
>
> *He acts, and is beyond action.*
>
> *Not hoping, not lusting, bridling body and mind,*
>
> *He calls nothing his own:*
>
> *He acts, and earns no evil.*
>
>> *Bhagavad Gita 4:19*

> *So the wise person (me?) is to melt in the flame of God's knowledge.*

Now I realize that I'm glad I got cancer. Really. If I hadn't, I wouldn't be here now. I couldn't be as detached as I am. The cancer showed me that nothing is important except God and family. It ripped away my attachments; it took away everything except Mom, and it gave Lauren back to me.

> *OK, there are a few other things I'm attached to. I'm really attached to Ben & Jerry's ice cream, but it hasn't been created yet in this time branch, so that's not an immediate problem.*
>
> *And my iPod; I really miss my iPod.*

I roll over on my side and look at Lauren, now awake, playing on the floor with a pile of stuffed animals. I am letting what I've read from the Gita wash over me. It feels as if the book has something to tell me, but I'm not quite getting it.

I close my eyes to chat with Swamiji.

> Swamiji: Namaste, old woman.

Namaste, Chatterbox-ji. Do you have time for an old lady's question?

> Swamiji: Please! I've been waiting for your question like a child waiting for Christmas.

(He giggles.)

Can you tell me please if there is a special verse in the Gita that can help me. I've read the whole book, but every verse seems as important as any other. My mind seems a muddle.

> Swamiji: Dear one, read the book over and over. Focus more on chapters two through nine. Each verse is a gem for a different moment. If I told you one of my favorite verses, you might focus on that and ignore others that are more important to you in the moment. In the Holy Qur'an it says, "God plans and man plans, but God is the best planner." Let God have his way with your study of the book and your life.

I feel as if I'm wandering. Surely there is a path I should be following to achieve detachment. Can you share your own path with me?

> Swamiji: No, we each have our own path to follow. It is the same with physical paths. If you were going to Chicago from where you live, and I was also going to Chicago, would it make sense for you to come first to India

so we could travel together? Imagine yourself walking to Chicago from Cleveland. Do you flog yourself each step of the way, saying, "I'm not in Chicago; I must be a bad person." It makes more sense to be joyful for each step, to celebrate your progress. So don't be in a hurry. Don't use someone else's path.

I don't understand being joyful at each step, when some of the steps in my life are so painful. I feel as if I might even be going backwards sometimes. I feel lost.

Swamiji: The Gita says to accept success and failure with equanimity. In order to do this we must understand that there is no success and no failure—not really. There is only progress.

In America, we are trained to avoid failure. We are punished for failure.

Swamiji: When an acorn becomes an oak tree, the acorn is completely destroyed. If you cut open an oak tree, you will not find the original acorn. To someone who only values acorns, the acorn's destruction is seen as a great tragedy. But without the new oak trees there would soon be no more acorns. The tragedy of the lost acorn is the source of more abundance. Look to the end of all things and you will see great abundance coming from small tragedies.

When I was dying of cancer, I saw my mother's sadness as a great tragedy. I've been hoping to change that. Should I have done nothing?

Swamiji: It is written, "What He hath willed hath been, and what He hath not willed, shall not be." When you first began this journey in the hospital, if you had asked me whether you should do nothing, I might have told you to wait and pray, but you acted, so we accept that.

Now, at this moment, and at each moment to come, we have other choices to make. We don't criticize our past decisions.

What actions should I take now?

Swamiji: You will know what to do if you simply act out of love. You are already doing this. Actions that come from love will lead to the smallest tragedies and the greatest abundance. Never act from fear.

Should I continue to wander in my mother's and sister's thoughts, trying to influence them?

Swamiji: Generally, no. Simply love them. You will find a time or two when it may be necessary to give them a little help. You will know when those times have arrived.

Thank you, Swamiji. Do you have time for one more question?

Swamiji: Of course.

I'm wondering about these time branches I'm creating. In the original life I was dying in 2018, in another my sister was killed by the Taliban. Is there now a woman dying in a hospital? Is a version of my sister dead in Afghanistan?

Swamiji: I can't tell you. I have no experience with these matters. Nor is there anything in our scriptures to tell me the answer. It may be that by going back in time you have destroyed the other time branches. But, looking at it another way, perhaps time branches can exist in parallel so in some way you are still the woman dying in 2018. My guess is that you have destroyed the other time branches, but I can't be sure. I hope you will learn the answer and tell me.

(He giggles.)

Namaste, Swamiji. Thank you.

Swamiji: Namaste.

I feel as if I've melted. It happens every time I talk to him. I'm only a puddle on the bed with no bones or muscles to get up. I drift off into a nap to try to recover.

I'm awake fifteen minutes later, lying on my side. Lauren is still playing with her animals. I tell her she's the best sister in the whole world. She smiles, brings a stuffed lion to my bed, then cuddles up beside me. I pet the lion for a few minutes while I replay Swamiji's instructions. I fall asleep. When I wake up, I hear Lauren laughing in the living room.

Chapter 12

May **1973.**

I didn't want to bore you with tales of the last few years, so I skipped ahead a bit. Lauren is now eleven. I'm sixteen.

Mom became a realtor last year and is making tons of money, but she works every day, sometimes until nine or ten. She seems to have found her untapped strengths, and really left her sense of inferiority behind her. Her clients really appreciate her and refer their friends.

As soon as she got the job, she traded her old Plymouth for a black Lincoln Towncar with air conditioning. Thank God! I'm sure if my Dad pulled up alongside her at a traffic light, he wouldn't recognize her. Not only is she dressed as a successful businesswoman, she wears makeup every day and has her hair professionally done. She looks great.

Speaking of Dad, he and Cynthia are still together. They married in 1970 and have a little boy. Lauren and I visit them several times each year, but not every month.

Last year we moved into a much bigger place, a beautiful, old, five bedroom house, near a country club in South Euclid. It's been quite a change in lifestyle.

We're going to better schools with friends that are more motivated.

Lauren and I are close. I couldn't ask for a better relationship with her. We're both busy with school, but able to take care of the housework so Mom is free to concentrate on selling houses. We can't do it all; a maid comes on Fridays to give the house a more thorough cleaning.

Now that I'm sixteen, I've been bugging Mom for a car, but we're still riding the school bus. There are lots of after-school activities that are hard to get to without a car. She doesn't say no, only, "I'll think about it."

* * *

I haven't forgotten about detachment, but I *really* prefer living in a big house with my own room. I enjoy looking into my walk-in closet filled with clothes from better stores. So, now I've got even more of my own stuff to get attached to. In my whole life, including the other time branches, I've never been able to spend so much money without worrying about it.

I even have an 8-track tape player and a growing stack of tapes!—Carly Simon, Roberta Flack, Barry White. I'm my own oldies station. But the tapes are huge! I should drop a note to Steve Jobs and mention what a great invention the iPod will be in thirty years!

* * *

It's Monday. The school bus drops Lauren and me at the corner near our house at 12:30. This afternoon there is some kind of teacher conference that we forgot about. When we get home, Mom's car is in the driveway, as is a Cadillac that I don't recognize.

As quietly as possible, we walk in the front door expecting to see some clients talking to Mom in the living room or dining room, but the house seems empty. We slink down the hallway to the rear of the house, thinking they might be in the kitchen having a cup of coffee. It's empty too.

Once we're in the kitchen, which is directly below Mom's bedroom, it's clear what's going on. Mom is making a lot of noise above our heads; she's clearly appreciating whatever Gordon is doing to her— screaming her appreciation in no uncertain terms.

"This is so gross!" Lauren scrunches her face and plops into one of the bar-stools at the kitchen island.

"Well, this is better than Mom coming home and hearing one of us going at it up there."

Lauren gives me a horrified look. I start pulling lunch from the refrigerator.

I make sandwiches while Lauren pours a cola for each of us. As we start to eat, there are footsteps on the hardwood floor above us, then quiet.

As we're finishing our sandwiches, Lauren asks, "What are we going to do? We can't go up to our rooms."

"We'll start our homework at the kitchen table. They should be down soon."

"This is so embarrassing. I don't want to be here when they come down."

The noise starts up again, this time with a soft head-board-banging rhythm. Lauren rolls her eyes.

"It's OK, Lauren. Mom will be embarrassed, but maybe we can have some fun."

"What do you mean, *fun*?"

"I'm not sure. We could pretend to not know what was going on, and see if they'll incriminate themselves."

Lauren and I are silently doing our homework when Mom walks into the kitchen wearing a robe that's barely closed. Her hair, which was so neatly arranged with hairspray when she left this morning, now forms a halo over her head as if she had her back to a hurricane. She doesn't notice us.

"Good afternoon," I offer as an opening volley.

Mom drops the bottle of club soda that she was taking from the refrigerator. It shatters on the tile floor.

"O my God!" she pants several times trying to get her breath. "What are you doing here?"

"The teachers had a thing this afternoon, so they let us out early. I'm sorry if we surprised you."

"Yeah. Right. It's OK. I ... uhh ..."

"Mom, we're fine. It sounded as if you were having a really good time."

A smile flickered across her face for a moment. "Yes. I mean, no. I mean ... Jesus!"

"I think it's gross!" said Lauren.

"Lauren, sweetie," says Mom, smoothing her hair while somehow making it worse. Now it looks as if the hurricane was coming from the side. "I wasn't expecting you. I didn't want you to ... to ..."

"Mom," I tell her, "we're all getting older. It had to happen sometime. ... So who is he?"

She gets a broom and dustpan and starts sweeping up the broken glass. "Gordon Whitely. He's a realtor in our firm. I think you've met him."

"Do you really like him? I mean, is it serious?"

"I believe so. Yes, I do like him. He's quite a gentleman."

"I'm glad you're having a good time, Mom."

"I still think it's gross," adds Lauren.

"I'm sorry, sweetie. This was our lunch hour. I didn't expect you girls for two more hours."

Gordon walks into the kitchen, crunching some broken glass beneath his shiny, black wingtips. He's dressed in a dark blue suit and looking the part of a successful realtor—tall and trim with gray temples.

"Good afternoon, ladies," says Gordon.

I stand up to shake his hand, "Good afternoon, sir."

He gives me a once-over that includes a momentary leer. Lauren seems too embarrassed to look up. She continues to read her book.

"I need to get to the office," says Gordon, gathering his car keys and kissing Mom on the cheek.

"I'll be there soon," says Mom to Gordon's smile and wave as he heads down the hall toward the front door.

As the door closes, I get a mop to help Mom clean up the club soda. "Get yourself ready for work, Mom. I'll finish this."

A week ago, I agreed to go out with Randy Larsen, a cute kid who lives on a farm seven miles east of us on US 322. He goes to Mayfield High a few miles away. I go to Brush High School in Lyndhurst.

Last month, some of Lauren's friends were going to a spring dance at Randy's high school, so she wanted to go. Mom insisted that I go along to chaperon.

The gym was filled with a combination of high school and middle school students, dancing to a band from the high school. They were trying to imitate *The Rolling Stones* and doing a really loud but terrible job of it.

Randy and I were leaning against the same wall near the refreshments table. I could see him glancing at me, but failing to dredge up enough courage to talk, so I moved closer to him and said hello. He opened up easily.

His mom had sent him to keep an eye on his younger sister, so we exchanged younger sister stories for a while. I was surprised; he was really interesting to talk to. He was dressed like a farmer so, due to my prejudices, I expected a limited conversation. When I mentioned that I liked ceramics and planned to go to art school, he said that he took two years of art in high school and really liked throwing pots. When we left the dance, he asked for my number. He has been calling me once a week since.

*   *   *

On a Saturday night a few weeks later, I am in our living room, waiting for Randy to pick me up. I put on some makeup, but didn't go all girly. I'm wearing jeans with a lacey blouse and a light jacket. If he wants his passions inflamed, he's going to have to use his imagination, I'm not giving him much to work with.

I answer the doorbell. Mom steps into the hallway from the kitchen to meet Randy who seems confident and polite. I'm told to be home by eleven.

We get in a red and white Ford pickup, about ten years old. The black rubber floor has an even layer of dust. The bed has a low pile of metal and wooden farm paraphernalia that I can't identify. It clanks and rattles as we drive along.

At the movies, we see *What's Up Doc?* with Barbra Streisand and Ryan O'Neal. I haven't seen it for forty years, so it's as if I'm seeing it for the first time—really hilarious. I expect Randy to make some kind of move on me, but he's a gentleman. About half way through the movie, I notice his arm is on the back of my seat, but he doesn't touch me. I'm guessing that his arm is probably asleep by now, but he can't figure out how to get out of the situation.

I can sense the hormones raging in my sixteen-year-old body. If that was all there was to the experience, I'd probably plant a wet kiss on him, but mostly I'm thinking like a fifty-something woman and the idea of romancing a seventeen-year-old boy feels illegal. I certainly don't feel sexy.

I reach behind me and pull his arm over my head, onto the armrest between our seats. I place his hand on top of my upturned palm and rub the back of his hand with my free hand. I hope that does it for him—a little encouragement without too much temptation.

He has really nice hands. They're big and calloused from working on the farm. My sixteen-year-old body imagines those hands roving over her breasts until my fifty-something mind tells the body to behave herself. The fifty-something sighs when she notices that the sixteen-year-old has created a wet spot in the crotch of their panties. She forces the attention of both of them back to the movie.

I haven't been thinking about my body much for the last few years, except for relishing how I look in the mirror—no wrinkles, flat tummy, perky boobs.

Sitting here next to Randy, aware of his physical presence, I notice my own body and its urges. I'm worrying a bit about Randy's needs.

As he drives me home, I'm considering a good-night kiss. If I wait for him, it either won't happen or he'll go overboard. I decide to take charge.

He pulls into the driveway and turns off the lights. He turns toward me with his arm on the back of the seat. He smiles. I return the smile, then scoot across the seat toward him, but not too close. I reach over, placing my hand on his cheek, then pull him into a quick smack. It's long enough that he doesn't feel cheated but brief enough that an old broad doesn't feel guilty.

I get out of the truck before he can react. "This was great, Randy," I say through the open window. "Call me again."

"I will. We'll do something next weekend."

"OK! See ya."

* * *

It's Sunday morning.

Mom is in her home office researching houses for her clients. Lauren and I are having breakfast in the kitchen.

"So, how was your first date with *Raannddy*?" she teases.

"It was good. The movie was so funny."

"Did you do anything? I mean, you know ..."

"Actually, we didn't go to the movies; we spent the whole time in the back of his truck. We took off all our clothes and did everything we could think of."

"Aargh! That's so gross!"

"I'm teasing. We held hands in the movies, and when he dropped me off I gave him a quick smooch, like I used to give you, only a peck."

"Really?"

"Yeah, I like Randy. I want him to really like me, not think of me as a sex toy."

Lauren shrugged. "I don't want boys kissing me."

"Wait a few more years, then see how you feel."

I notice that there's coffee in the machine. I pour a cup of coffee for Mom. She's been in her office upstairs for a few hours; I'm sure her cup is either empty or cold.

I carry the cup up the stairs, then walk past her bedroom to her office. The door is open.

"I thought you might need a fresh cup." I set the cup in front of her and stand next to her rubbing her shoulders.

"Oh, thank you! I've got to go out in a few minutes to show these houses to some clients."

I pick up a stack of notes that she's made from the listing service. "Those are some big houses! These people must be loaded."

"They said they wanted something around two million. Can you believe it? Most people ask for so many square feet or so many bedrooms. What kind of people ask for a set price like that?"

"They might want to impress someone who lives in a house that only cost one million dollars."

Mom laughed, "That's probably it."

"Where are these houses that are worth two million?" I say, setting Mom's notes on her desk.

"Not in neighborhoods around here! There are some estates in the hills east of town—really big houses with lots of land. It makes me really nervous showing expensive houses. I have no idea what rich people consider important. One buyer rejected a fabulous house because the wine cellar wasn't to his liking."

"I'm so proud of you, Mom. You've come so far in just a few years."

"Thank you, but I'm scared to death. If I sell one of these houses, my firm gets about sixty thousand. If I don't sell one, it's as if I've cost the firm that money. I've never been responsible for such large numbers."

"The clients love you. You'll do great."

"I tell myself that, then I remember that my dad worked his whole life for less than a hundred thousand. Who am I to make sixty grand for driving some rich guy around the countryside for a day."

"You don't get all that, right?"

"No, I get about half. Still ..."

"Speaking of Grandpa, you could consider getting him an expensive birthday present. I saw him looking at a fishing pole that was over two hundred dollars. I could see from the way he handled it that he loved it, but he put it back, shaking his head."

"I will do that."

"And you could buy me a Camaro."

"No."

"Mom, Lauren and I have all this stuff to do after school; Lauren's in gymnastics twice a week, and I was in that play. We have to get rides from other people, or walk to a freezing bus stop and wait for the bus."

"I know. I'll think about it. Let's talk about it during the summer."

"Sell the house, then we'll talk."

* * *

It's seven o'clock Sunday evening. Lauren and I are in our rooms. Mom explodes into the foyer, shouting for us. Lauren and I run downstairs wearing shorts and t-shirts. Gordon is standing behind Mom.

"They signed the contract! Go get dressed. I'm taking us all out to dinner."

"We kinda already ate, so can we come along for some dessert?"

"That's good. The reservations are at eight. Hurry and get dressed.

* * *

In Gordon's new Cadillac on the way to the restaurant, my mind drifts back to my date with Randy in his old pickup, and my feeling that I'm dating a child. I'm sitting behind Mom so I have a good view of Gordon, of his smiles as he turns to talk to Mom, of his graying temples.

Right now, I could see myself getting hot and bothered with Gordon. I feel as if I'm his age. I wish I could be more relaxed about Randy's age, but I can't. I am who I am. Being with Gordon would be even weirder, since I'm in this teenybopper body. My mind is out of sync with Randy and my body is out of sync with older men.

By eight we are seated in a fancy Italian restaurant with white table cloths and crystal glassware. Mom insists on ordering a salad for Lauren and I, so we can all have dessert together.

"Your mother," says Gordon, "is about to enter the million dollar club."

> *The old fart is talking to my boobs. Does this bother me? Not like it used to. But then, it's been a few years since I've had boobs for men to talk to.*

He continues after a sip of wine, "This is a really big deal. Only agents who sell a million dollars worth of property in a year get in. She'll have a walnut plaque over her desk at work. Each fall, the company takes the club on a week-long cruise to the Bahamas."

"I've never been on a cruise," says Mom.

"You'll have to get used to it, Lottie. This is only the beginning. I'm sure you will be in the club every year from now on."

The server brings the food which interrupts the conversation for a minute.

As he moves away, I ask, "Mr. Whitely, why is Mom such a successful realtor?"

"Hmm. ... People can probably sense that she's honest and has their interest at heart. Some realtors are like car salesmen—a bit too hungry. Your mother is relaxed and looks after the client's needs without worrying about the sale. People can sense that."

"They can?" asks Mom.

"You're great. And after you have some more experience, you'll be more confident, then you'll be even more relaxed. You are destined for greatness."

"You go girl!" I say, then realize that it isn't a '70s expression.

"What?" says Mom.

"Just saying I'm proud of you, Mom."

After dinner, Gordon orders a slice of Torta della Nonna for each of us—five bucks a slice! I'd never heard of it, a custard pie with pine nuts and almonds.

> *It's so great to have money!*
>
> *I know. I know. Detachment!*
>
> *Got it!*

*   *   *

June 5, first day of summer vacation.

Lauren and I are sleeping in. Mom left for work around eight. I'm awake but don't feel like getting up. Yesterday afternoon I sensed some unhappiness from Lauren. I asked her about it, but she said everything was OK. I don't believe her, so I open a channel.

I thought so; she's been feeling lonely at school because she hasn't made any good friends since we moved here. She doesn't seem terribly unhappy. I'll send her a hug and break the connection.

I'm on my back, reading *Jonathon Livingston Seagull* when I hear Lauren wake up. I walk next door and stand, leaning against her door frame. She's sitting with her legs dangling off the side of the bed. I sit down beside her.

"What?" she asks.

"I want to read something to you."

She leans her head on my shoulder and yawns.

"Listen, 'It was morning, and the new sun sparkled gold across the ripples of a gentle sea.'"

"I've never seen the sea."

"I haven't either. This book is so beautiful. It's really about overcoming limitations, about going past our limiting thoughts. ... Here it is! This is the quote I really wanted you to see, *'You have the freedom to be yourself, your true self, here and now, and nothing can stand in your way.'* I believe the book is about not allowing other people to define who we are, or what we can become."

"I like the pictures."

"You want to read it? I'm finished with it."

"Yeah, OK. But now I'm hungry."

"Maybe after you've read the book, we could talk about it. Let's go have breakfast. ... How about pancakes?"

* * *

After breakfast, Lauren is washing the dishes. I'm standing beside her, drying them.

"This could be a really boring summer," I say, "unless we can think of something to do."

"I wish we were still living at the apartment. I had lots of friends there."

"Mom's too busy to be running us back and forth to Cleveland. And the buses would be a hassle."

"I know. ... It's too far to hang out with those kids," says Lauren.

"Let's find something new to do near here. What sounds like great fun to you—swimming, dance, music? We need to think outside the box."

"What box?"

Another '90s expression ...

"Never mind. ... I mean, we don't have to do the same old stuff. Let's think of something really exciting, then look for a way to make it happen."

"Here's the newspaper ..."

I notice a small ad for a ceramics store a mile away that has pottery classes. Lauren doesn't want to do pottery, but I write down the woman's number for later.

After we flip a few more pages, there is an ad for a dance studio in the same shopping center. There are several classes for different kinds of dance. Lauren seems mildly interested.

"Let's walk down there now," I suggest. "They'll be open by the time we get there. We can check it out."

It is a pleasant sunny day in the mid-seventies. We walk through our subdivision, then along Mayfield Road to the shopping center. We check out the ceramics studio first. The woman who runs it says that they don't have a set class schedule; I can come anytime and she can help me whenever I need it.

We go a few doors down to the dance studio. The owner is a cheerful and athletic woman who shows us a book with pictures of different dance styles. Lauren says she likes the look of Jazz, so we sign her up for a month, three times per week. She can easily handle the cost from her allowance, if Mom doesn't want to pay for the lessons, but we are sure she will.

*   *   *

The summer flew by. Lauren and I walked to the shopping center Monday, Wednesday and Friday afternoons. We walked home each day with Lauren covered with sweat and me speckled with clay.

* * *

On a Monday in late August, we were walking home after our classes. Lauren wasn't talking, which was unusual.

"You OK?"

"Yeah, I'm fine."

I opened a channel to her as we walked along in silence. I was too curious to wait until we got home.

Ah! One of the girls from her class kissed her in the bathroom. Lauren liked it. She likes the girl too. I wondered when this would happen.

I broke the connection. I put my arm around her shoulders to give her a quick hug as we continued along Mayfield Road.

At home we both shower, then meet in the living room to watch *Love American Style*. Lauren still seems distracted.

"You know you can talk to me about absolutely anything, right?"

"Sure, I know."

"Did something happen today during dance class? You were really chatty before class."

"Yeah, something good happened, but I'm not ready to talk about it. Can we talk later?"

"Anytime."

Mom called to say she was going out with Gordon after work and for us not to wait up.

* * *

That night Lauren and I watch *Monday Night at the Movies*, then get ready for bed. I'm lying in bed with the lights out when Lauren calls me softly through the common wall.

"Cailyn, are you asleep yet?"

"No."

"Can I come talk to you?"

"Sure."

I slide over so she can lie down beside me. I put my arm around her and she lays her head on my shoulder as she did when she was little.

"What's going on?" I ask.

"Today, during Jazz class, Michelle fell and hurt her knee. She was crying a little and went to the bathroom. I went in after her to see if she was OK. I put some cold water on a paper towel and washed her knee for her. She had stopped crying by then. When I stood up I put my arms around her just like you and I do sometimes. It felt really good to stand there and hold her. When I let go, she pulled me back to her and kissed me really hard. I was so shocked."

"How do you feel about it now?"

"I don't know."

"Did you like it? Do you want her to kiss you again? Or maybe it feels like ..."

"Oh, I did like it! I felt really warm and excited. I definitely want to kiss her again."

"Did you feel at all that you were doing something wrong?"

"A bit. I mean, I know girls, older girls, kiss boys that way, but it seemed weird for two girls to do it."

"OK. I guess you know that some people believe that it's very wrong for two girls to kiss each other—and the same for two boys?"

"Yeah."

"I think you should do what feels right. Today you want to kiss Michelle. In a year or two, you might want to kiss a boy the same way. You may find that a special boy makes you feel better than kissing girls. You may decide that you like girls better. It doesn't matter."

"Really?"

"Mom and I will love you whatever you decide. We want you to be happy. But other people will treat you badly if they know that you like girls better, so when you're doing stuff with a girl, you need to do it in private. The same is true if you're with a boy, but it's more important when you're with another girl. People don't want to see any couple smooching and touching in public."

"Have you ever done stuff with a girl?"

How do I answer that? Not in this time branch?

"Not yet, but I haven't done anything with a boy either."

"You kissed Randy."

"Yeah, but only a smooch, nothing to get excited about."

"Would you like to kiss him hard, the way Michelle kissed me?"

"Umm ... no, not really. I think I will later, when I

know him better."

Or when he's twenty-one!

"How old is Michelle?"

"I think she's thirteen or fourteen."

"You could invite her over some night. We could rent a movie."

"Rent a movie?"

"Sorry, I meant watch a movie on TV. We need to meet some friends who live near us. Where does Michelle live?"

"Close, I think. I'll ask her."

Chapter 13

June, 1976.

I thought you'd prefer that I skip over some teenage angst, so I jumped ahead again.

In the last few years, there have been some exciting events around the world: the Vietnam War ended, as did Nixon's presidency, the oil embargo raised gasoline prices, and inflation is high. At the moment we're in the middle of the Ford-Carter presidential campaign.

Lauren has several good friends now, including Michelle, but they're not a couple. Michelle is a bit of a flirt with several girls. Mom and Gordon are definitely a couple. I'm sure they would have moved in together by now if it wasn't for Lauren and me. Mom has been going on cruises with Gordon and the other Million Dollar Club realtors every November. She returns home mellow and suntanned.

Randy and I are still dating, but he's seeing other girls which gives him an outlet for his rapidly expanding passions. At least he's shaving every day now, so I'm starting to look at him with some passion and without any guilt. We're both in college at Case Western; he's studying agricultural science and I'm in art history. He'll be a junior in the fall; I'll be a sophomore.

Mom finally bought me a Camaro. I wanted a red one, but she said that red cars get more speeding tickets, so I settled for a blue one.

I know—detachment, detachment. I'm working on it. How can I practice detachment if I don't have any attachments to detach?

*   *   *

Mom, Gordon, Lauren and I sit down to our weekly meal together. We've been doing this every Sunday night for a year or two. On all the other nights of the week, Mom is with Gordon or with clients, sometimes both. She usually sleeps over at his house. I'm OK with it. Lauren says it's gross.

Gordon and I are from different planets. He's a Republican's Republican. I'm in art school. None of my friends talk like him or even discuss the things he does. Gordon never talks about the subjects that interest my friends and me.

I would be truly shocked if there was a single Republican among my fellow students or my professors. For us it's peace, love and beauty. For Gordon it's money; if you want peace, love and beauty, you only need enough money.

So we have a running battle on Sunday nights. I've got quite an advantage having lived, once upon a time branch, through the next thirty years. I know who wins in November. Tonight, as during the last several weeks, the conversation is about the election.

"If you want inflation to come down," Gordon says, poking the table top with an index finger, "you have to get rid of government regulations, so businesses will prosper. Then you'll have more competition and prices will come down. Carter wants to maintain the natural gas price controls, for God's sake! Let the damn markets decide."

I should make a bet with him about the outcome of the election. Hee! Hee! Bad Cailyn! Bad!

"You can't forget that Ford pardoned Nixon," Mom tells him. "After all the things Trickie Dick pulled, he should have spent some time in jail."

"That will probably hurt Ford in November," admits Gordon, "but Nixon did some great things; he opened up relations with China and the USSR including treaties limiting nuclear weapons. Our country is safer because of him."

"It seems to me," I offer, "that Republicans are about business only. They want the government to benefit the corporations. Democrats want healthy businesses, too, but they want the people protected from the greed of corporations. They're for people first, business second. The Republicans want it the other way around. ... So given that choice, I'll take the Democrats."

"We can't afford a government that is everyone's rich uncle," says Gordon. "The government budget would grow and grow until we're all broke."

"I believe that's an assumption," I tell him. "Other countries have more of a people focus, and they don't go broke."

"Not any country I'd want to live in!"

"OK," says Mom, "let's change the subject. How's school, Cailyn?"

"Good, I'm only taking one class this summer, ceramics studio. I'm working on some ceramic sculptures. There are only ten of us in the class, so we're becoming good friends."

Gordon rolls his eyes ever so slightly. I smile at him. I know he wants to continue the political discussion.

"Lauren," I continue, "has a Jazz recital coming up at the end of the month."

"You're all invited," says Lauren, beaming. "It's on Saturday, the twenty-eighth."

"We'll certainly plan on being there," says Mom, glancing at Gordon who smiles.

Small talk continues for the remainder of the meal, then Gordon says his good-byes and leaves.

The three of us girls start cleaning the kitchen.

"I need to tell you, Cailyn, that Gordon and I will be working for the Ford campaign, starting this week. We've agreed to go to the Republican headquarters in the evenings to drum up support for Ford. I need you to back off on politics when Gordon is here."

"But Mom, you don't believe that stuff, do you? Are you really a Republican?"

"I've never really thought much about politics. I believe in people first, as you said, but everyone at work is saying that the Republicans will bring more prosperity overall. I feel as if I have to go along. Apparently everyone at the firm and most of our clients are Republican. Your father has always been Republican. I would support the Democrats, if I was still working at Helen's store, but I'm enjoying making a good living. I couldn't have paid cash for your Camaro if I was still working at a store selling crystals and incense."

"OK, Mom. No problem. I won't start it, and if he does, I'll just smile. Don't tell him that I'm working for the Carter campaign."

"Oh, Cailyn! You're not! Are you?"

"Just kidding."

While I was sick in 2016, I read books by the dozen. One of them—what was the name of it?—talked about how the Democratic administrations have actually outperformed the Republicans in terms of increasing stock values, growing industrial output, reducing debt, adding jobs—any way you want to measure the economy. But that information wasn't available in 1976. Too bad; I'd like to pepper-spray Gordon with those statistics until he's rolling on the floor, screaming for mercy.

Just to irritate him, I would go work for the Democrats, but I know Carter is going to win Ohio without me. When Carter wins in November, that will be far more irritation than I could create by working for the enemy.

* * *

It is Wednesday afternoon. Lauren and I should have left for her dance class five minutes ago. I'm ready. She isn't. I'm standing in the doorway of her room, jingling my keys.

"I just don't have anything to wear. All my leotards have runs. I want unitards anyway. I need some new sweats; these are grungy."

"Well, I understand that you want some new clothes, but let's make the best decision we can with what you have. There isn't time to go shopping."

Lauren fusses, but finds some clothes that will work.

"Can we go to Macy's on the way home? They've got some great outfits for Jazz. All the girls are wearing them. Can we, please? Please? Please?"

"Do you have enough money?"

"No. Can you lend me some, then Mom will pay you back."

"Let's call Mom and get her OK first."

* * *

July 11, 1976.

I'm in a cemetery, standing next to Mom and Lauren. Across an open grave, sitting on two rows of folding chairs, are Randy and his sister Becca with some of their relatives. Between us are two caskets, covered with flowers.

Their parents' minister talks about how "They're with the Lord now."—whatever that means. Randy and Becca both look stricken. He has his arm around her shoulders.

Randy's mom and dad had been coming home from a July fourth party when a drunk suddenly swerved into their lane, hitting them head-on. Randy's dad died immediately. His mother lived for a few hours.

* * *

A month later, I give Randy a call on a Saturday morning. I ask him if he'd like to go somewhere. He says no, but he asks me to come visit him.

I drive out Mayfield Road until I reach the gravel drive that drops down into the little valley that is mostly occupied by their farm. It's been sunny the last several days, so the Camaro kicks up some dust as it accelerates down the hill, coming to a stop next to Randy's house.

There are two farm houses; one belonged to Randy's grandparents until they passed away, the other to

Randy's parents. Four barns of various sizes store equipment and supplies.

Randy is repairing a fence where the horses have nibbled the top board in half. I walk over, looking for some way to help.

"Good morning. It seems your horse liked the taste of that board."

"He did at that. How are you today?"

"I'm good. Is there anything I can do to help?"

"You've come just in time. Please hold this end of the board while I nail the other end."

The fence repaired, we walk to the house. He throws the old board on the woodpile on the way.

"You ready for some coffee?" he asks.

"You bet."

"Come on in."

I sit at the kitchen table while he pours two mugs. We sip for a few minutes. I've always felt awkward when talking to people who are grieving. I'm hoping he'll start the conversation. He does.

"My parents left the farm to Becca and me, jointly. She decided to take grandpa's old house for herself. It's somewhat nicer than this one because grandma had it remodeled a year before she died. I kinda like this house though—with it's lived-in look. It's where I grew up."

"It's a warm house. It feels as if there has been a lot of love here."

"Yeah, you're right; there was a lot of love."

We're quiet for a few minutes while we sip. I walk to

the fridge to look at the photos. I recognize Randy's mom and dad; I don't know the other people. The photos show that his family knew how to laugh together.

"Your mom and dad seemed to enjoy their life. Am I right?"

"You are. Dad could be stern, but Mom always filled our lives with her love. She wasn't educated, but she sure knew how to make people feel treasured."

"I suspect that she taught you some of that."

"I hope so."

Randy joins me at the fridge. He studies the pictures as if it's the first time he's seeing them. I step behind him and put my arms around his waist. He's a head taller than me. I hug him tight while pressing my cheek against the back of his shoulder. We stand that way for some minutes while he continues to look at the photos.

He pulls my arms loose, turns and kisses me. It wasn't just a peck this time.

* * *

Sunday, November 7, 1976, the first Sunday after the election. Carter won Ohio and the nation.

But you knew that.

Gordon is despondent at dinner. This is the first time the four of us have been together since the election. Mom is making small talk. Lauren is indifferent. I'm smiling, at least on the inside. I hope my expression isn't a gloating one.

Gordon puts down his knife and fork, then holds his head in his hands as if he could begin weeping,

"I can't understand it; Ford took the West; Carter took the East and the South. How did that damn peanut farmer take Ohio? I never heard anyone say they were voting for that idiot."

"Well, dear," says Mom, "maybe the Ohio farmers wanted to elect another farmer. I don't know."

I start to say something, but take another bite of salad instead.

"Well, we'll just have to start now to work on the 1980 election!" says Gordon, stabbing the table with that same index finger, "Ohio has to go Republican next time."

> *Yeah, it will. Reagan carried almost all the states in 1980, including Ohio. Gordon seems to really enjoy abusing the table, doesn't he?*

Gordon takes a bite of steak. After it's half chewed, he says, through gritted teeth, "If Ohio goes Democrat in 1980, I'm moving to Idaho."

Mom doesn't look up from her plate; she continues eating. Lauren, with a bland expression, is watching the other three faces. She doesn't seem to care one way or another.

I'm struggling; I'm determined not to smile, or laugh. I like Gordon; he's really been good for Mom, and to Mom. I suppose she is worrying about him moving to Idaho, and whether she would go with him. If he leaves Ohio, I know it won't be because of the 1980 election.

* * *

Lying in bed that night, I decided to chat with Swamiji. It's been over a year since I talked to him.

Swamiji: Ah! old woman, (He giggles.) I was wondering when you would call on me. Here I am, tears running down, thinking, "When will she call? When will she call?"

(I laugh.) Well, Swamiji, you can always call me if you really get lonely.

Swamiji: I've been watching you, old woman. You are winning your battles with the self. You haven't needed my help.

Do you ever need to talk?

Swamiji: Not really. I'm surrounded by people all day. I give them love. They give me love. It is enough. But talking to you is a special treat; you are extra sugar sprinkled on my cake.

I'm still struggling with detachment, Swamiji. I read the Gita and try to make good choices, but it is difficult.

Swamiji: You're doing well. It is more difficult for people who live complicated lives, like yours. My life is simple. I only own a few robes and some books. If I owned a house and a car, I would worry about their maintenance, insurance, all that. You must find a way to use the things of this world without feeling that you own them. It is the sense of owning that brings worry.

My mother is slightly wealthy now. She and my sister are becoming materialistic. Is this a problem? Should I intervene in some way?

Swamiji: You can intervene, but not by pushing

them away from their possessions. Praise their spiritual qualities. We must increase the spiritual rather than decrease the physical. As the spiritual life improves, physical needs fall away naturally. You must do this in your own life as well. You are attached to your new car. It is a beautiful car. You cannot think, "I must not care for the car." That thought will cause you to grow even more attached. You should increase your love of God, increase your service to your family and others, then the car will take its proper place automatically.

Sometimes I beat myself up for failing to detach.

Swamiji: That is what I mean about pushing material things away. You are on the right path. You are not at the end, but you are wandering toward it. Don't flog yourself; you can be joyful at every moment, even at times of error, or anger, or selfishness. When our minds are content with our overall progress, we are always joyful, even when we aren't perfect.

Are you perfect, Swamiji?

Swamiji: All I do is sit here smiling at everyone. How much trouble can I get into? (He giggles.) No, I am not perfect. Our minds always want to drag us down to a physical level, even the minds of swamis. My mind tries to convince me that I am someone special. ... I'm being honest with you. ... I am only perfect in the sense that when I have these ego thoughts, my buddhi immediately sees the lie and throws a bucket of cold water on those thoughts. If I were perfect the thoughts wouldn't be there. I am told that even the greatest saints have these thoughts, so I am content with the path I'm on, and I know that I haven't reached the end of my path.

You are so helpful to me, Swamiji; why don't you speak to your students in India, so you can help them as you're helping me?

Swamiji: I have tried that; I spoke to people in the early years of being a monk, but I found that their minds corrupted my words.

In India we talk about how our ego colors our thoughts—distorting them. The students used their colored impressions of my words to stay where they were on the path. Their progress stopped! When I speak to you, my buddhi is speaking to your buddhi. Our minds are not involved. This is what I try to do with these students who are sitting around me now while I'm talking to you. Hopefully my buddhi sends love to their buddhi and gives them energy to move along the path—wherever they are on the path and in whatever direction they are supposed to go next. I don't make that decision for them. I'm not perfect enough for that. But I can love them—almost perfectly, as I love you. My love attracts them to the end of their paths.

Your blessings to me are almost too much to bear, Swamiji. I love you very much.

Swamiji: I know. (He giggles.) Your love is even more sugar for my cake. I am getting fat from so much sugar.

I'm falling in love with a man, someone who goes to my college.

Swamiji: I know. He's an excellent man. You've made a good choice.

Any advice for me?

Swamiji: With him, old woman, don't be a monk.

(He giggles.)

I won't. Bye for now.

Laughing, I break the connection.

Chapter 14

I'M JUMPING AHEAD AGAIN, this time to March, 1980. Nothing surprising happened during the last few years. Mom and Gordon are still together, still working for the Republicans and still going on cruises every November.

Everyone is confident that Reagan will be elected in November so Gordon is quite relaxed with no plans to move to Idaho.

Lauren will finish high school in June. She is still studying dance and teaches classes for the younger kids. Mom bought her a little white BMW last year. It's two years old, but it looks new.

Randy and I are a couple; he's sleeping only with me— as far as I know. We both graduated from college. I've been renting one of Randy's barns as a ceramic studio for the last year. It's perfect for my work and it gives us a chance to see each other through the day. He seems happy. I definitely am.

I would move in with him, but Mom doesn't want Lauren living in the house by herself.

* * *

April, 1980.

Randy and his sister Becca are throwing a party at their farm. It's a spring break party for those of our friends in graduate school who didn't go to the beaches.

Lauren and I arrive at eight and park between two of the smaller barns. The sun has set, but the sky still has a pink glow above the western hills. We lean against the fender of my car for a moment, surveying the scene. The stereo is playing on the porch of Randy's house. There are two kegs of beer on Becca's porch. On both porches are tables with snacks. It's a warm night and smells of freshly cut grass. Randy must have mowed the lawn today.

"I'm going for a beer," says Lauren. "Is that OK?"

"Fine. Just don't get drunk and puke in my car."

Randy's house is a large, old, two-story farmhouse, painted white. On three sides there is a deep, wrap-a-round, wooden porch with no railings. I walk across the sloping lawn to where he's sitting on the edge of the porch, drinking beer with two of his friends.

Because of the height of the porch, Randy's knees are level with my shoulders. He introduces me as his girl-friend. I smile, then excuse myself to get a beer. On my return, I climb the porch's six stone steps to sit beside him. The sports-centered conversation is a bit on the male side for me, so I focus on Lauren talking to Becca on the other porch. Since I'm not needed for Randy's conversation, I open a channel to Becca.

She's chatting Lauren up. I always thought that Becca was gay. But this is the first time I've opened a channel to check her out. She's really attracted to Lauren. I suspect that Lauren is attracted too. Becca is a beautiful redhead. Whatever they're talking about, it's making Becca happy.

I break the connection and scoot closer to Randy. As my arm touches his, he reaches over to hold my hand. Another car arrives. There are about twenty people now, wandering between the beer and the snack tables, dancing barefoot in the grass, or smoking marijuana in a small circle near the stereo on Randy's porch.

Over the next two hours, more people arrive. Most are from the ag-science department, but I invited a few from the art department—people I thought would mix with the ag-science students without being snobbish.

A few minutes before eleven o'clock, I notice a second-floor light in Becca's house turn on. Looking around, I don't see Lauren or Becca anywhere. It's tempting to open a channel to Lauren, but I resist it.

Randy and I spend the evening sipping beer and talking to everyone. I'm impressed with his ability to make everyone feel welcome and valued. I especially like the way he listens to people without arguing. So many young men are in a perpetual pissing contest, but Randy will just smile and let a boast pass without attempting to outdo the other person.

After midnight, Lauren and Becca join us on the porch, holding hands. I can tell Lauren is rattled. I don't need to open a channel to see that.

On the way back to our house, I decide to be nosy. "You seem to like Becca."

"Jesus! She is something."

"So you think you could fall in love with a farm girl?"

"I could fall in love with that one. She made me feel ... I've never felt like that before."

"Could I give you some advice?"

"Advice from the straight girl ... OK, but just a little."

"Don't make it only about sex. Becca is a beautiful person. I know her pretty well. Since I've been hanging out with Randy, she's become a dear friend. I believe the two of you could be a couple, but you would have to live in her world. I can't picture her living in yours. So—I'm only suggesting—you might spend some time working with her on the farm. It would give you a chance to see who she really is."

"Look, I just want to have fun. I'm not looking for happily ever after."

"Except, ... Becca could be your happily-ever-after and you could blow it if she feels that she's only a sex toy to you. I don't want to be too pushy; just think about it."

"OK, I will. I will. ... I really do like her."

* * *

November 9, 1980.

This Sunday dinner reminds me so much of our dinner four years ago; we're all sitting in exactly the same places as before. Even the food is the same; I remember we were having steak that night, too.

But tonight Gordon is beaming. Reagan got fifty-one percent of the popular vote and ninety percent of the electoral college. The Republicans won back the Senate and made some gains in the House of Representatives. His threat to move to Idaho is a distant memory. He doesn't poke the table once during dinner.

"Next time, we'll take back the House. We've got momentum now. In 1982, after two years of Republican progress, the public will be clamoring for more."

> *Yeah, right! Reagan turned out to be a spendthrift. We went right into a recession. The 1982 election reversed the Republican gains of 1980. The man was an idiot. Revered by the right-wing, but still an idiot.*

Before I can think of something nasty to say about Reagan, Mom changes the subject, "What did you ladies do this weekend?"

"I spent the weekend working on Randy and Becca's farm," says Lauren. "They finished the harvesting last week so there was lots to do—cleaning the equipment and getting it ready for winter."

I can tell from Gordon's scowl that he's aware of Lauren and Becca's relationship. I'm surprised Mom hasn't said anything to her.

"I was out there, too. I'm getting several pieces ready for an art show down in Columbus."

"It's getting so cold," says Mom, "will you be able to work in that drafty barn this winter?"

"We've lined the barn with heavy construction plastic to keep out most of the drafts. The pot-belly stove and the kiln keep it pretty toasty."

"It sounds a bit primitive," says Gordon.

"Oh, it is; it is. But it fits the art. I'm working in clay, part of Mother Earth. It would be different if I was a painter doing portraits in a loft downtown. You and Mom should come out sometime in the next few weeks, so you can see the pieces before I take them to Columbus."

"... and we could show you around the farm," adds Lauren.

"We'll try to do that," says Gordon.

Mom smiles, "Jesus! How did you girls end up on a farm? In all these years I never once thought of you as farmers."

"Well, we're only apprentice farmers," I tell her.

"Have you and Randy talked about getting married?" Mom is smiling again.

"No, but I believe we're wandering in that general direction."

"What about you, Lauren," says Gordon, "do you have a special guy?"

"I'm still looking," says Lauren with a chilly tone.

*　*　*

December, 1982.

Since last spring, we've all changed our sleeping arrangements. Lauren and I have been living with

Becca and Randy in their respective houses. Gordon moved in with Mom after he sold his house, making a fortune on the deal.

This particular December morning, I'm in my barn cleaning things up after spending the last month getting ready for an alumni art show at Case Western. It's really cold out and starting to snow. A few flakes are blowing in the gap between the barn doors.

Lauren comes in with two mugs of coffee. "I need to talk."

"No problem."

We sit in two ratty overstuffed chairs that had been in Randy's living room until Murphy, his rottweiler, took his claws to them.

"I'm two months pregnant," says Lauren, looking down into her mug.

I had just picked up the coffee mug and almost dropped it. "Jesus! How the hell did that happen?"

"That's what Becca's going to want to know."

"Yes, and what's the answer."

"You know Brian, the other dance teacher?"

"The Brian who's gay?"

"Right. We were all alone after everyone left and we were in the back, both excited from the dancing and all hot and sweaty."

"So you both decided to have a little straight sex to celebrate being hot and sweaty."

"Something like that. It was such a stupid thing to do."

"And you haven't told Becca yet."

Tears are slipping down both cheeks. "No, not yet."

"OK, give me until tomorrow to think about this," I tell her, "then you and I will talk again and come up with a strategy."

"Maybe you can come up with a way that I never have to tell her."

"Do you want to have an abortion? That would be one way of never telling her."

"No," she gets up and paces, "no, I want to have the baby. I'm pretty sure of that. I feel bad enough already. If the baby died, it would be even worse."

"Good. Let's talk tomorrow morning."

* * *

That night, after Randy falls asleep, I open a channel to Lauren.

She's not yet asleep. She's worried, cuddled up with Becca. I let time slip forward watching the emotional explosion as Becca finds out about the pregnancy and the two of them struggle through the aftermath. Time continues forward for a few years so I can see how it all turns out.

> *But I'll keep it to myself for now so I don't spoil the story for you. It's not only that; the time branches*

can change sometimes when I put my two cents in.

I need to run this by Swamiji.

> *Swamiji: Old woman! You've found one of those times when you need to meddle.*

> *Yes, Swamiji. My gay sister is pregnant and is afraid to tell her girlfriend about it. I'm telling her that if she's truthful, her girlfriend will accept the situation. Am I right?*

> *Swamiji: You're correct, my dear. Truthfulness is the foundation of all the other virtues. If we lie, even if the other person believes us at first, we have lost the relationship because the buddhi of the other person knows the truth. You have looked at the future of this situation?*

> *I have. It seems to work out for the best.*

> *Swamiji: I will send your sister a telegram in the morning. It will say that heaven wants this child to be born. It will be a blessing to her and her partner. She mustn't worry about anything.*

Lauren looks pretty sad when she comes to my studio the next morning. She slumps down in one of the chairs with her elbows on her knees and her forehead in her palms.

"I hope you came up with something because I sure didn't," she says between her wrists.

"I did, but you're going to have to trust me."

She looks up. A tear is running down one cheek.

"If you say anything dishonest to Becca, it's going to make it worse. So you must be absolutely truthful. Before you say anything at all, you need to decide what is true for you."

"What are you talking about?"

"I think it's true that you really adore Becca and want to spend the rest of your life with her."

"Right."

"Are you really sure? Completely sure?"

"Oh, I see what you mean. Yes, I need to consider that some more. I think I do, but I could be more sure."

"OK, do that. So, if that's true, then you tell her that you love her more than anything, that you want to spend the rest of your lives together, but you made a silly mistake that you're really sorry about, and you hope she'll find a way to forgive you."

"That's your plan?"

"Believe me, it will work."

"How are you so sure?"

Damn! I can't tell you that.

"Randy and I will be on your side. We both believe you're good for each other. We've talked about it."

"Not about the baby!"

"No! ... No, I haven't said anything to him about the baby, but we've talked about the two of you, and how you love each other. Once you've told Becca about the baby, I'm sure that we'll both urge her to see the positive side. Once she gets over the shock, she'll start to see that you'll be raising a baby together. That's pretty cool, right? Lot's of lesbians look for ways for one of them to get pregnant. You simply leaped over that step with Brian. And it isn't going to happen again, so she doesn't have to fear the future. She will forgive you if we can replace her fear of the future with confidence in you as a partner."

"I think I've learned my lesson about casual sex with men."

We hear a car in the driveway. I open one half of the barn door. I smile when I see the Western Union emblem on the side of the van. The driver walks toward us. Lauren looks over my shoulder.

"Cable for Miss Lauren Whittaker."

"That's me."

Lauren tears open the envelope and reads the message while the van returns to the highway.

"It's from that swami that we met years ago when we were kids! It says that heaven wants my baby born and everything will be OK. Jesus! How the hell did he hear about this?"

"They told us that the swami knows everything. I guess he does!"

"I want to calm down before I talk to Becca."

"That's good. I'm sure she'll be pissed in the beginning, but she'll come around. Allow her to be angry for a time, and forgive you at her own pace. Don't try to change her anger. It will go away on its own."

Lauren hugs me for a long while. It was like when we were little except now she's taller than me. She gathers the coffee mugs, then walks to the barn door.

She pauses for a moment at the open door, looks back at me with snowflakes swirling around her. "Thanks, Sis."

"Don't forget: allow her some time for anger."

* * *

The next evening, Randy and I are in the kitchen eating dinner when Lauren opens the kitchen door holding a small duffel bag. Tears are running down. I pull out a chair for her, then fix her a plate of food and a cup of coffee.

"I haven't said anything to Randy;" I tell her, "you should fill him in."

"I'm two months pregnant."

"Oh?"

"Becca wants me to sleep over here."

"I don't understand," says Randy. "Do you have a boyfriend now?"

"No! Not at all! I love Becca. I don't care for anyone else."

"Well, then how ..."

"I was staying late at the dance studio with Brian, and we just got excited and did it."

"I thought Brian was gay."

"He is. We were changing our clothes in the back. We're often nude around each other because—well, it never had any effect before. We were just being silly, then he got a boner for some reason, and we thought, *What the hell?*"

"Maybe Brian isn't as gay as he thought."

"Well, maybe, but I am! It wasn't what I expected. I thought it would be interesting to do it once, but I won't be doing it again."

"So what did Becca say?" I ask.

"She wasn't as furious as I thought she would be, but she's mad and hurt. She cried and said that I should sleep over here for a while."

"Randy," I say while I rub Lauren's shoulders, "I talked to Lauren about this yesterday. She really adores Becca and wants to spend the rest of her life with her. She doesn't ever want to have sex with anyone else, male or female. So I hope you will encourage Becca to forgive her."

"I'll go talk to Becca after dinner."

"Don't push her, though. It won't hurt for her to sit with her anger for a while. Just tell her that she is the love of Lauren's life. This was only a one-time mistake."

"Is that true, Lauren?" asks Randy.

Lauren nods her head, tears flowing freely.

* * *

A week later, Lauren is still staying with us. She's been hanging around with me during the day in my studio when she's not teaching dance classes. Becca hasn't spoken to her since the revelation. Randy tells us Becca is calming down but isn't ready to talk about it.

The three of us are cleaning up from dinner when Mom arrives. The snow must be falling heavily out there; she has quite a few flakes in her hair and on her shoulders. Her eyes are red.

I give her a hug, then take her coat.

"Have you eaten, Mom?" I ask.

Mom sits down at the kitchen table. "I don't want anything to eat. Thank you."

"What's going on?" I start moving the dirty plates from the table.

"Gordon left me."

"Jesus! What happened?" says Randy.

"What do you think? A younger woman ... not much older than Cailyn. It doesn't take much to attract these old men."

Lauren puts her arms around Mom's neck from behind, then kisses her cheek.

"I needed to tell someone. He moved out today. I understand he moved into her apartment."

"Is there anything you need—anything we can do?" I ask.

"No, dear. It'll be OK. I'll have a cup of coffee if you've got one, then go back to my empty house."

"Are you sure? You could stay here tonight," I say as I fix Mom's coffee. I look at Lauren because she's sleeping in the only spare bedroom. She shrugs her shoulders.

"I'll be fine. I've been through this before."

Randy is sitting in the chair closest to Mom, looking from face to face. He turns his chair and leans toward her, taking her hand, and says, "It's his loss, Mrs. Whittaker. You're a beautiful woman. He'll be sorry before long."

"Thanks, Randy." She takes the cup of coffee from me. "I'll drink this, then be on my way."

*   *   *

After Mom leaves, Randy goes over to check on Becca. Lauren and I sit in the living room watching TV until nine when Randy returns. We all decide to call it a night.

Randy and I get in bed, then hold each other while talking about the other three members of our little family. Randy tells me that Becca mentioned tonight that she had thought about having a baby with Lauren, but in a few years. She wouldn't have chosen for it to come now, but the timing isn't terrible. She still feels afraid that she can't trust Lauren. I ask him if he thinks I should talk to Becca. He says I should wait a few days.

We make love slowly on our sides. It's my favorite

way; he seems to like it too. He's very gentle, kissing the back of my neck and swirling his fingers over my breasts. He's barely touching them—the slightest tickle. The climax for both of us is just as gentle. I feel him fall asleep.

I open a channel to Becca. It's time to cheat a bit.

She's sad and fearful, but she loves Lauren. I can feel the longing for a future together and the fear that Lauren may not be ready to settle down.

I send her my love, and keep sending it until I'm sure she's feeling it. My love seems to strengthen her enough that the fear starts to fall away. I send her some thoughts about her new daughter *(Yes, it's a girl.)*, visions of she and Lauren laughing with a beautiful little girl who is getting dressed for a party. I send her the thought that Lauren loves her more than anything.

Then I break the connection so I can open one with Lauren.

I can feel that Lauren is slightly conflicted. A part of her still wants to have a few more years of dating before settling down. Most of her mind is getting used to the idea that the baby is coming and will demand all of her time regardless of her future with Becca.

Her mental universe is expanding from looking solely for her own entertainment to caring for Becca and the child. She knows that, with her new family, she's going to have all the excitement and love she could possibly want, but it's taking her some time to give up the last vestiges of her old desire to be a wild and crazy girl at parties.

I send her the same images that I sent Becca—of the two of them with their beautiful child. I send her my love and what I sensed of Becca's.

As I experience these images myself, I become aware that I am so ecstatic that I'm almost bursting. The man I adore still has his arm around my waist. My precious little sister is in the next room with my new niece inside her, and I have another sister asleep in the house across the driveway. I will be an aunt in seven months! I send my joy to Lauren, then I reopen the channel to Becca to let her taste it too.

As I close Becca's channel, I remember Mom, so I reach out to her. She's asleep, but I can feel her abandonment. She really loved Gordon. Before I lose my buzz, I send her the joy that I'm feeling about the four people who are on our farm. Then I decide to connect with Gordon.

I have trouble connecting with him. My unhappiness with his treatment of Mom is making the connection difficult. I have to work on forgiveness first. I think about how everyone is on their own path and that I can't judge his path, that whatever he did to Mom is part of his path and hers. His actions are only a little tragedy that will move everyone toward their ultimate goals—to greater abundance.

Eventually I connect with him.

I'm feeling something beyond his attraction to this other woman—something financial, it seems. I sense worry. I was planning to send him images of drowning kittens if he was having sex with his new girl, but he's not having a good time at all. He's worried about Mom. I stick with him a while to see if other feelings are there, but it only seems to be worry. I close the connection.

*   *   *

I call Mom the next day at her office, but she's taking a sick day. I reach her at home.

"Have you talked to Gordon since he left?"

"No, I really don't want to talk to him."

"Mom, I think something else is going on. I have a feeling that it's more than an old man attracted to a younger woman. I believe he's in some kind of financial deal that's gone wrong. You know how I get these feelings about things. This time it's a bad feeling."

"O God! I hope you're wrong. Two months ago, Gordon and I both invested in a shopping mall deal. Between us we put in four million. I had to take a second mortgage on the house. It was too good to pass up; when the property is operating, we were told to expect a return of twenty million in the first five years."

"Please call Gordon and find out what happened. I'm sure there's something he hasn't told you. There might be some action you need to take."

"OK, dear. I've come to trust your feelings about things. I'll call him today if I can find him."

*   *   *

I was working in my studio the next afternoon when Lauren came in with two coffees and a smile. We sat down in the ratty chairs.

"I'm feeling a lot better," she says.

"I was hoping you would be better today. Have you talked to Becca?"

"No, not yet, but I talked to Brian today. We had a few minutes after our classes were over."

"Really?"

"I told him I didn't want anything from him—just wanted him to know. He was shocked but really cool about it. He said that he'd like to be involved—as much as Becca and I want him to be. He's really a great guy."

"Yeah, I like Brian."

We sipped coffee while we listened to a Joni Mitchell song playing on the radio.

"How are you feeling about Becca?"

"I think ... no, I'm sure that I'm ready to commit to her and the baby. I only needed to grow up a little."

"You know, a big bouquet of flowers might be appropriate. And a card that says, 'I love you.'"

"I will."

"The phone's right there. Call now."

Lauren nods. She picks up the yellow pages that are underneath the phone on the table between us. The table, the book and the phone are covered with a film of dried clay and glaze. She calls the florist, then hangs up with a smile.

"You have to do something; you can't simply wait for

her to come to you. You need to show your love every couple of days until she feels comfortable with you again."

"You're right. You're right."

"I know this is a tough time for you, but I gotta tell you, I'm bursting with happiness. I'm going to be an aunt! I'm so excited about this baby. You, Becca and I are going to have such a good time spoiling her."

"It will be fun, won't it? — assuming she'll take me back."

"She will. Does Mom know about the baby? Or about the spat between you and Becca?"

"No, I haven't said anything yet. I thought with Gordon ..."

"Right, I thought the same. There's no hurry."

*   *   *

A week passes. Mom drops into my studio around noon on a Thursday, two days before Christmas. She looks cold, frazzled, worried.

"You were right, dear. I finally cornered Gordon. He told me he couldn't face me. There are financial problems—big ones. It was Gordon who talked me into that damn shopping center deal. The developer collected fifteen million from six different investors, then disappeared. No one knows where he is."

"Where does that leave you?"

"I'm going to sell the house and move into an apartment until my finances improve. I'll be OK. I still have a good income."

"Do you have to sell the house?"

"I could probably get by, but the house reminds me of Gordon. I'd rather get rid of it, pay off the mortgages and start over. I'm going to move to another firm, a bigger one that does more commercial properties. Gordon's going to stay where he is. I told him I didn't want to work at the same firm."

"Will you be OK financially?"

"Sure, I only need to sell a few properties."

Christmas was weird. Randy, Lauren, and I went to Mom's house for breakfast and gifts. Randy and I left Lauren there, then went to Becca's house for lunch. Along with our gifts for Becca, we brought Lauren's gift, a necklace that matched one of Becca's favorite blouses. She sent us away with a sweater for Lauren.

Another two weeks passes. Since Lauren is starting to show, we decide to tell Mom, so we invite her and Becca to dinner at our house. The night before the dinner, I connect with Lauren, Becca and Mom to bathe them in my love and joy.

Mom arrives at seven. Becca joins us a few minutes later. It's a bit tense. This is the first time Becca and Lauren have been in the same room since the night Lauren moved to our house. We seat Mom, Randy and

Becca in the living room until Lauren and I get the table set. I see Lauren glancing into the living room, trying to make eye contact with Becca. Becca seems to be ignoring her while making small talk with Mom and Randy.

Lauren announces that the table is ready. We're having salad and lasagna with home-made apple pie for dessert.

As the meal comes to an end, Lauren says, "Mom, we've got some big news for you."

"Really?"

After a long pause for effect, Lauren says, "You're going to be a grandmother."

Mom looks at Randy then me. "Cailyn?"

"Oh, no! Don't look at me. I'm the auntie!"

Mom pushes away from the table a few inches. She's still smiling but puts both hands to her mouth in shock. She's looking rapidly between Becca and Lauren. "Well, this is a surprise! How did you go about it? I mean, did you go to a clinic or something?"

"It was an accident," says Lauren.

Becca is staring at her plate, moving the last bits of food around with a spoon.

Mom tilts her head and looks at Lauren, "An accident?"

"You know Brian at the dance studio."

"Yes."

"He's the father. We were acting silly one night and got carried away."

Mom looks at Becca who doesn't look up.

"Well, that was a really stupid thing to do, Lauren. I'm sorry; I know that's blunt, but I'm not quite over Gordon running off with his little tramp. I hope you haven't hurt Becca as much as Gordon hurt me."

"I have hurt her, and I feel rotten about it. I adore Becca more than I thought was possible, and I hope she can forgive me."

Becca, neither smiling nor frowning, glances at Lauren, then back to her plate.

"These things take time to get over," says Mom. "I hope you'll both continue to cherish each other while the hurt passes. It will pass, Becca."

I bring out slices of apple pie for everyone then serve the coffee.

"How far along are you?" asks Mom.

"This is the twelfth week," says Lauren, sneaking a glance at Becca.

"You must be starting to show a little."

Lauren stands up between Mom and Becca so Mom can feel her belly. While Mom is holding her hand against Lauren, Becca puts her hand there also. I notice Becca smile at Mom, then turn back to her pie.

* * *

Two weeks later, after a month of my nightly connec-
tions to send love and healing to Lauren and Becca,
they come over at dinner time to announce to Randy
and me that they had patched everything up that
morning. Lauren had returned her stuff to Becca's
house during the day. There were hugs all around.

"We've decided that I won't go back to the dance
studio," said Lauren. "I'd have to quit soon anyway
with the baby. I talked to the owner today. She's
already got someone to replace me."

I set two more plates at the table. "You will be pretty
busy when the baby arrives."

"Yes, Becca and I feel that I should be a housewife at
least until the baby is in school."

"I agree," I tell her. "You and I can care for the baby
and keep up the two houses. That will free Randy and
Becca to focus on the farm."

Before I sit down to eat, I walk behind Becca, give her
a hug around the shoulders and a kiss on the cheek.

Chapter 15

M<small>AY</small>, 1983.

Randy and I are watching TV. It's about eight-thirty when the phone rings.

"Hello."

"Cailyn," says Mom, "I've been arrested. They arrested Gordon too."

"What the hell did you two do?"

"It's not what we did. Apparently that bastard that swindled us committed several felonies before he skipped town. Since we were his partners in the development project, they're holding us responsible. Apparently he swindled more people than we thought."

"Why aren't they going after him?"

"They're working on it, but they still haven't found him. Apparently, according to the law, we're as guilty as he is because we made it a partnership and not a corporation."

"What do you need us to do now?"

"We need you to bail us out."

* * *

Around midnight, Randy and I flop into bed after getting Mom and Gordon released. Randy is immediately asleep. I open a channel to Swamiji.

Dear Swamiji, I have a problem; I hope you can help.

   Swamiji: Old woman! I felt your unhappiness so I was expecting your call.

My mother was arrested because she was a partner with a man who committed some felonies without her knowledge. The man has disappeared. Can you help find him?

   Swamiji: Let us keep talking. I will find him. How are your sister and her baby?

They are very well. The baby will be born in July.

   Swamiji: And her relationship with her friend; that is all healed?

Yes. They are back together.

   Swamiji: Your mother has regained her happiness, except for this little legal problem?

Yes, she is at peace and overjoyed about the new baby. She visits us often.

   Swamiji: That is very good. ... My dear, tell the police that they can find your mother's partner in Vanuatu.

Where is that?

   Swamiji: It's an island northeast of Australia. They won't be able to arrest him, however. I'm sorry. Nevertheless, your mother will recover from these difficulties.

I know. Thank you, Swamiji.

* * *

The next morning, I call Mom from the studio to tell her that her partner is in Vanuatu. She wants to know how I know. I tell her to chalk it up to psychic powers. She says she'll pass that on to the detective so she can check it out.

I can't work—not today; at least I can't be creative. I piddle around cleaning up and organizing some supplies that have been sitting in a corner of the barn since they were delivered a month ago.

Lauren comes in for our morning coffee. She still has her slender dancer's body except now she looks as if she swallowed a whole watermelon without chewing.

She squats down in a chair. "I feel like I'm having triplets."

"You look really healthy. What has the doctor said about your weight?"

"We're right where we should be."

"Great!"

"What's wrong, Cailyn? You look worried."

"Yeah, there was some excitement last night; Mom and Gordon got arrested."

"O God! What's that about?"

I filled her in.

"Do we know what her partner actually did? — besides swindling Mom and Gordon, I mean."

"He was selling additional partnerships. He only needed ten million to buy the land, but he collected over twenty-seven million from fifteen partners who all thought they would be twenty to thirty percent owners. Since Mom and Gordon attended some of the early meetings, encouraging others to become part-ners, they were seen as being in on the scam. Two weeks ago, their partner left the country with all the money without ever buying the land."

"Is there anything we can do?" Lauren asked.

"I don't see how. Any James Bond types among your friends who could go to Vanuatu to get Mom's money back?"

"Vanu-what?"

That night, Mom called to say that her real estate license had been suspended pending the outcome of the trial; so was Gordon's. She would be free on bail until then. The trial was scheduled for September.

Chapter 16

July 2, 1983.

Becca calls at two a.m. to say they're heading for the hospital. I get dressed and follow them in my car. I decide to let Randy sleep.

I call Mom at seven to tell her we are at the hospital. Lauren still has a long way to go; she's not dilated much.

Mom arrives before ten. Becca and I are in the room with Lauren. Becca is the birthing coach, but there's not much to do but wait while Lauren makes steady progress.

The labor proceeds with no drama until Jessica is born at ten-seventeen that night; she is twenty inches long and a healthy seven pounds, four ounces. We are all exhausted. Judging by the bags under our eyes, we all look as if we had just given birth.

Becca kisses Lauren after wiping the sweat from her face. Lauren smiles and says, "If we decide to do this again, you get to be the mom next time."

* * *

Mom moves into Becca's guest room to help out for a while. Between the four women, Jessica gets plenty of attention and Lauren gets some rest. It's great having Mom close by again.

Toward the end of Jessica's third day in the wider world, Mom comes into the studio with two mugs of coffee. She looks askance at the ratty chairs with their even coating of beige clay dust. I throw a clean drop-cloth over one of the chairs so she can sit down.

"I'm planning to return to my apartment at the end of the week," she says.

"We seem to have everything under control, but it's been really great having you here."

"I've got to get back to town and work on our defense. I've been talking to Gordon and our attorney. At the moment, it looks like we have some jail time ahead of us."

"Jesus! Why?"

"We can't prove that we weren't in on the scam. If we hadn't attended those meetings when our partner presented the deal to other people. One of the people he swindled has some important friends including a judge—our judge! The attorney is sure the judge is going to want a pound of flesh from someone."

"If you're convicted, will it be hard to get your broker's license restored?"

"Absolutely! If we had robbed a bank, we'd have a better chance of getting it back. Being convicted of real estate fraud is a killer. Gordon is saying we would be better off declaring bankruptcy, then starting over in some other field. Maybe I'll go back to selling crystals in Helen's shop."

"Wow! I never thought that would happen to you."

"I didn't either. I really liked the life that Gordon and I had before he ran out on me. I could kill him for messing things up so badly. I never would have gotten involved with that damn shopping center if it wasn't for him pushing me. *Oh, we're going to make so much money!* Right! By the way, the detective told me they found our partner in Vanuatu, but that country doesn't have an extradition treaty with the U.S., so there's nothing she can do."

"If you declare bankruptcy, will they take everything?"

"No, but they'll take almost everything. I wanted to tell you that I've been squirreling away money for you and Lauren. The accounts are in your names. I wanted to make sure you had some kind of a legacy when I died, or, in this case, went to prison. I'll bring the paperwork out to you in the next few days so you'll have the account numbers. There are two brokerage accounts, one for each of you."

Chapter 17

Mom is crying. "I thought I could handle this, Cailyn, but I can't. I'm so humiliated."

Mom and I are talking in her cell at the county jail. Her trial ended yesterday. Tomorrow, she'll be transferred to the Ohio Reformatory for Women in Marysville for six months, then she'll be on parole for another year. It could have been worse.

She continues, "I know I didn't really do anything wrong, but I feel so stupid, so ashamed. I don't know how I can face people. I really enjoyed our house; how can I go back to living in a cheap apartment like we did before? How am I going to live in one of these damn cages for six months?"

I wish there was something to say that could make the hurt go away.

"Mom, we're all on your side. Randy and I, Lauren and Becca—we all love you and look forward to having you with us again. I hope you'll find that, when you return, some of the friends you made through Helen's shop will love you as much as ever. If they don't, then it's their loss."

"I can hear that, and I want to believe it, but when I imagine meeting the other people who lost money—

they were our friends!—I want to kill myself. I can't face them; I can't."

"Mom, I don't have any magical advice, but I think if you stick with your meditation throughout the next six months, you'll find some peace, and that will put the money problems in the right perspective. You'll have lots of time to meditate."

"I can't imagine peace—not now."

We sit side by side, holding hands until a police-woman comes and tells me I have to leave. We hug each other one last time. As I walk with the officer to the steel door, I hear Mom blubbering as she did at my bedside in 2018.

* * *

After Randy falls asleep that night, I connect with Mom as I lie in bed.

What I see in her is what she told me in the jail cell: embarrassment and shame. I send her some love and an image of Lauren and Becca laughing with Jessica.

I decide to connect with Mom every night while she's in prison, to send her some love, if nothing else.

* * *

On Friday, Lauren and I are allowed to phone Mom for three minutes. We ask her if the other women are threatening her at all. She tells us that the other women aren't a problem. There are no nasty crimi-nals; they're mostly prostitutes, drug users and people who got caught passing bad checks or committing minor fraud. While she can't really be friends with any of them, at least none of them are being aggres-sive. She's says she's meditating a lot every day.

$*\quad*\quad*$

I wake up early Saturday morning. Randy is still beside me. I connect with Swamiji before getting out of bed.

Dear Swamiji, I was just waking up and thinking about my mother.

Swamiji: Yes, Old Woman, I am delighted to hear from you. It is late at night here.

I was wondering if you can do something for my mother while she's in prison. I don't know what is possible.

Swamiji: You are sending her loving messages every day?

Yes.

Swamiji: I believe your love will do the most good, but I will connect with her while she is meditating. I will see that she has some deeper experiences so she will feel encouraged to meditate more.

That sounds perfect.

Swamiji: How is little Jessica?

She is a delight. I adore being an auntie.

Swamiji: When she is an adult, music will be important to her. Begin to play excellent music in her room to help develop her innate skills.

That's wonderful. We will.

Swamiji: When you next talk to your mother on the telephone, ask her about her meditations.

(He giggles.)

I will do that, Chatterbox-ji. Namaste.

* * *

Lauren and I call Mom on Friday for our three-minute chat. Mom is in a state; she's complaining about everything and everybody. It's seems as if everything is the opposite of what she wants and nobody is willing to help her change things. We can't get a word in; she is ranting a litany of complaints.

Our time is almost up. I ask, "Mom, how are your meditations?"

This seems to flip a switch in her.

"Never better! Twice this week I've been drifting in an ocean of bliss."

Lauren says, "You deserve bliss, Mom."

We end the phone call with the usual salutations.

* * *

The next morning I connect with Swamiji.

Namaste, Swamiji. I spoke to my mother yesterday.

Swamiji: Namaste. I was hoping you'd call.

My mother seemed to be angry about everything except her meditations.

Swamiji: I see her anger. The meditation is increasing the contrast between her interior life and her exterior life. She'll get past this. She is seeing the negativity in herself projected onto other people. In time she'll realize that it is her own negativity that is causing her to see the bad qualities in others. In time she will be projecting her joy onto others.

Am I projecting my negativity onto others?

Swamiji: We all do that, my dear. We must learn to recognize when we are projecting so that the thoughts can dissipate. It is important that we don't act on them.

Thank you. I hope you'll keep visiting Mom during her meditations.

Swamiji: I will, but now I must sleep.

Namaste, Swamiji.

Swamiji: Namaste.

*   *   *

Lauren and I continue to call Mom every week. She isn't always ranting, but it's clear she's unhappy with the prison and the other prisoners. I connect with her every day, either at night before falling asleep or in the morning if I wake up early.

I'm beginning to see a slightly different story when I connect with her. It's not so much the demeaning procedures, the facilities or the prisoners; it's her sense of self, her hatred of the lower middle class home she came from, the frustration of not fitting in with Dad's friends and family. The prisoners remind her of where she came from; they are her class of people.

Swamiji is right; Mom is projecting her negative stuff onto others. I decide to add something new when I connect with her. Along with the love, I add the thought of everyone being one. "Ye are the waves of one sea." as someone wrote.

Our individual bodies are only as unique as a wave

that appears on the surface of an ocean for a few seconds. The "something" I use to move in time and space has to do with that ocean, that underlying ... what? Field? It felt like a lake, but what if it is really an ocean from which everything else arises? If our bodies and our thoughts are all just ripples on the surface of that ocean, how do we relate to another person's actions or thoughts? How can we get angry with them if we know that we aren't separate from them? Why do we get angry?

I think I need to connect to myself and dig deeper into my own consciousness. Can I do that?

*   *   *

Our next phone call with Mom is no better, but it is different somehow. I'm connecting to her every day to work on these ideas of relating to others as if they are part of the same whole that she is. I'm working on myself, attempting to do the same thing. It feels as if it's working.

*   *   *

The following Friday, the call is different. She brings up her great meditations first; she's really been enjoying them. She tells us that she found that her anger at other prisoners was really anger at herself.

"Mom, how can you tell that your anger is really at yourself?" I ask.

"I've been talking to these women about their lives. Not all, but some grew up in neighborhoods like mine. I married your father, and he gave me a sense that life could be more pleasant. But these women married people from the neighborhood, some of them hooked up with petty criminals. Their lives went downhill instead of up like mine. I could have ended up exactly like them if I'd made the same choices. I find that I'm really grateful to your father. That's a bit of a shock after all these years."

Our time was up.

"Love you, Mom. We'll call you next week."

*   *   *

The next Friday morning, I decide to connect with Swamiji before talking to Mom that afternoon.

Good evening, Swamiji; can we talk?

> *Swamiji: Namaste. I'm still awake.*

My mother is making progress. She tells me she has sympathy for the other prisoners now.

> *Swamiji: The love you are sending her each day is having an effect.*

Is there something else I can do for her?

> *Swamiji: Be patient with yourself and with her. You are both learning detachment. It takes some time.*

Is there no other lesson that I could offer her when I connect to her?

> *Swamiji: Tell her that joy only exists in the present moment. The past is for sorrow, resentment and anger. The future is for fear and worry. Live only in the present moment. We make our plans for the future, but when the future arrives, we accept the results without complaint. Remember the acorn and the oak tree. We must look to the end of things and not obsess about our little tragedies. They will ultimately bring abundance. However, we can*

only experience joy in that abundance if we are able to live in the moment. It is possible for the abundance to arrive, but we fail to recognize it due to worry or fear of the future.

I will spend the day trying to understand that for myself. I love you, Swamiji. Sleep well.

Swamiji: Namaste, Old Woman.

* * *

At three p.m. Lauren and I call Mom. Jessica is being verbal so we put her on for a minute so Mom can hear her cooing.

"How are you feeling now?" I ask. "Is your life there smoothing out a little?—getting used to things?"

"Yes, I believe it is. I'm meditating and reading constantly, trying to find peace."

"Any new insights from all this meditation?"

"It's hard to explain. I sit in my cell and go through my body asking it how it feels. How does my right hand feel? How does my left hand feel? — like that — so after going through my body, I end up feeling OK. You know, all the parts are reporting back that things are working pretty well."

"We're really looking forward to you coming back home," says Lauren. "I've never imagined how hard it would be to have a long-distance relationship with you."

"I know. I've never been more than a few miles from you girls."

"We're going to come visit you soon, Mom," I tell her.

"I'll be here," she laughs.

Chapter 18

NOVEMBER, 1983.

On a Saturday, Becca, Lauren and I take four-month-old Jessica to visit Mom in Marysville. It's a three hour drive from the farm.

The prison is a minimum security facility, so we are able to have a relaxed visit. I worried we might have to talk as they do in the movies—through a glass with telephones, but it is nothing like that.

After initial kisses and hugs, Mom takes Jessica, then we all sit down in a large room that wouldn't be out of place as a high school cafeteria except for the guards in each corner. We sip soft drinks and furtively glance at the other families who are meeting around us.

"Any news from the outside?" asks Mom.

"The farm did really well this year," says Becca.

"Randy and I are great," I tell her. "He's relaxing after the harvest and I'm working in my barn every day."

"How are you feeling, Sweetheart?" Mom asks Lauren.

"I've never been happier. I didn't realize being a mom would be so much fun."

"I hope it's always this much fun for you," says Mom, smiling as if to say just wait.

"I know. It'll get harder when she starts to move around."

"... and starts talking back to you," Mom adds.

We stay with her for thirty minutes, then the guards tell us we have to go. Other families are waiting for our table so they can visit their inmates.

* * *

That night, as Randy and I get into bed, I'm thinking about Mom's future after she gets out. She could probably work in Helen's shop if she wants to, but she won't be able to afford a decent apartment on the pittance that Helen could afford to pay her.

"Randy, how would you feel about putting a trailer on the farm for Mom to live in? I was thinking about that level spot behind the big barn."

"Well, let me look into that and discuss it with Becca. Let's talk about it some other time."

"Good night, Sweetheart."

"Good night."

We turn off the lights and cuddle while we fall asleep.

* * *

I don't bring the subject of Mom's trailer up again. I know Randy by now; he won't forget, and he'll bring it up when he's ready to talk about it.

Two weeks later, I'm in the kitchen frying eggs and bacon for breakfast when Randy, dressed for a day's work, comes in and pours himself a mug of coffee.

"I thought about a trailer for your mother, and I

talked it over with Becca since it's her decision, too."

"and ..." I ask, with my back to him, as I slide his breakfast onto a plate.

"The thing is, I think we should be married before we do something like that."

That turns me around. I expect to see him face to face, but I'm looking down at his upturned face.

"Will you marry me, Cailyn?" he says from his kneeling position.

> One of the advantages of this time branching business is knowing the future of questions like this, so there's no point to adding any drama, either for his benefit or for yours.

"Randy, nothing would make me happier. But, I want to wait until Mom is out of jail."

"Of course. And about the trailer—Becca and I thought we should wait to talk to your Mom about her needs before we buy anything, so let's put all that off for a while."

"Did you talk to Becca about us getting married?"

"She is overjoyed. She already thinks of you as her sister."

"I feel the same way."

Chapter 19

March, 1984.

Randy and I are driving his pickup to Marysville to pick up Mom when she is released later today. This route from Cleveland to Marysville must be the flattest piece of land in the country. You can see to the horizon between the barns on farm after farm. It's probably one of the few places where you can sense the curvature of the Earth without being at the top of a mountain.

Inside the prison building, after going through two security checks, we're shown into a waiting room with concrete walls, plastic furniture and magazines from the Carter administration. About an hour later, Mom comes through a steel door with a big manila envelope and a paper shopping bag with some clothes and books.

After hugs and kisses, we walk to the parking lot in silence. I want to talk to her, ask questions, but I can sense she is experiencing something that shouldn't be disturbed.

In the car, I'm sitting in the middle. Mom remains quiet, appearing lost in thought as she looks out the passenger-side window.

"Are you OK?" I ask, holding her hand as we pull onto

the highway.

"It's so strange to be out driving around. I can't imagine how people react after they've been in jail for years. I feel as if I don't belong out here."

"We didn't ask you what you wanted to do when you get home. Would you like to stay with us?"

"No, I don't want to be a bother."

"But Mom, you don't have any food at your house. Stay with us tonight."

"Alright, thank you."

We stop in Mansfield for dinner at a family restaurant. While we're waiting for the food to come, I ask, "What's the next step for you?"

"I'm going to sell the house first, then probably declare bankruptcy. I'll have to talk to an attorney and see what they suggest."

"I know this might sound strange, Lottie," says Randy, "but, if you want to, we could put a trailer behind the barn and you could live there pretty cheaply. You'd have your own electric, gas, and telephone. Our well has enough capacity for you to tap into our water system. You think about it. We really want you to live on the farm with us, and it'll keep you close to Jessica."

"Besides, Mom, we're getting married soon. There might be some more grandkids to be close to."

"Really? Are you pregnant?"

"No, not yet."

"When is the wedding?"

"We wanted to decide that after you got out," said Randy. "We're thinking sometime in May."

"Thank you for waiting. I'm sure any Saturday will work for me. I've never filed bankruptcy before, but I'm sure nothing happens on the weekends."

"How are you feeling, Mom? I mean—about losing Gordon, the house, the career?"

"I was pretty sad when I went to jail; that was really humiliating. But it gave me all that time to consider who I am—who I want to be. As I told you, some of the women in there were a lot worse off than me. I found gratitude. What I'm most grateful for is my two daughters, and Randy and Becca, and Jessica. Most of the women I talked to didn't have a family to look forward to. They had families but with so many problems. They weren't always looking forward to getting out."

"We're grateful for you, Mom."

Chapter 20

THAT NIGHT, as Randy is watching the last few minutes of a basketball game on TV, I'm sitting up in bed thinking about my grandmothers, Mom, Jessica and the babies that Randy and I will have. I write in my diary:

6 March 1984

Part of me connects to them;
A time, my time,
merges with theirs;
More than that though,
a soul path,
like DNA,
connects women forgotten
with women yet to be.

Randy comes to bed. I set the diary on the nightstand. As I snuggle up to his back, I'm struck by the thought of our bodies, and the babies these bodies will make someday soon. I'm feeling so blessed in that moment,

I want to talk to Swamiji.

> *Swamiji: Old woman! I'm thrilled to hear from you.*

Namaste, Chatterbox-ji, I wanted to thank you for all your help. Everyone in my family is happy.

> *Swamiji: You have all found joy in the journey!*

I have been thinking about our joy. The TM people often talk about enlightenment. I'm so happy now; I wonder if this is enlightenment.

> *Swamiji: Enlightenment is not a goal; it is an infinite process. You are enlightened compared to where you were last year; you are not as enlightened as you will be soon. We never reach the end. As we move along this path, we live increasingly in the moment. There is no anger or regret about the past because those small tragedies led to the current abundance. There is no fear of the future because we know that future tragedies will only lead to further abundance.*

Is that all there is to enlightenment?

> *Swamiji: As we move along the path, living increasingly in the present, we find it easier to follow the instructions of Jesus, "Do unto others as you would have them do unto you." As we understand the relationship between tragedy and abundance, we are able to joyfully serve others with no expectations. When we are in that state of joy, with confidence in the future, God's love is able to flow through us to others.*

Are you enlightened?

> *Swamiji: Old woman, remember it is a process, not a goal. You and I are each moving along*

our separate paths. It is possible that you are more enlightened than I am. Don't be surprised that I say that. I am only a yogi who knows some teachings from the scriptures, and a few tricks about communicating with people. If I were in your place, perhaps I would not have done such a good job of serving my mother and sister. It is easy being a monk; all I do is smile and meditate. You women with families have the hardest job. To serve your families with joy and wisdom is a great accomplishment.

I read the Gita and I feel that I must learn much more before I am enlightened. I feel ignorant.

Swamiji: The Gita and the other scriptures have been made overly-complicated by men who wanted to be admired for their knowledge. In the Qur'an it says that truth is a single point which the ignorant have multiplied. What is that single point? It is simply the Golden Rule. When we are detached enough, mindful enough, then we can apply the Golden Rule in every interaction, even in every thought. In the Gita it says that to an enlightened soul, all the scriptures have the value of a small well in a land flooded with water. The scriptures are important because they guide us to that point. However, they are not that point. We must not make a god of the scriptures.

You answer my questions so simply. How can you make the complicated so easy?

Swamiji: It is written that the wise man needn't know many things, only fewer things that aren't true. I know what isn't true. When you ask me these questions, I only have to peel off the thin outer layer of error to reveal the simple truth inside. You will learn to do this very quickly, then you can answer my questions. (He giggles.)

Oh, Swamiji, I am so grateful that you've been my friend through all this. Namaste.

Swamiji: Namaste, old woman. Namaste.

* * *

June 1984

So many movies end with a wedding scene with everyone dancing. The camera pulls back from the beaming faces, then cranes up and wide to an overhead shot of the whole party with the sun going down in the background.

We were going to have such a wedding out on the lawn in front of Randy's house, but it was drizzling, so the wedding was on the wrap-around porch. Afterward we all moved inside for cake and champagne. It was simple. There were no disasters. No one got too drunk or otherwise embarrassed themselves.

Right now we're on our honeymoon in Pensacola Beach, Florida, a beautiful strip of sugar white sand in which to wiggle our toes. I brought my diary along.

* * *

September 1984

It's about nine in the morning on a beautiful fall day. I carry two mugs of coffee up to Mom's new trailer. I knock, then stick my head in the door.

"Mom, are you decent? I've got some coffee for us."

"I'll be right there."

I sit down at her new dining room table, putting the

coffee mugs on coasters.

"I was just finishing my meditation," says Mom as she emerges from the hallway. "It was glorious."

There's a knock. Lauren comes in with Jessica on her hip. Mom holds out her hands. Lauren gives the baby to Mom, then kisses her cheek.

"How's the trailer working out for you, Mom?" I ask.

"I believe this will be perfect. I have the quiet I think I need right now, and I'm close whenever one of you needs me."

"You were going to talk to Helen about working in the shop again. How did that go?"

"She doesn't need me. She hired someone else a few years back and that person is working out well. I'll find something to do in Mayfield. I don't need much. There must be a similar store I can work in."

* * *

October, 1984

Two days ago, I found out that I'm pregnant.

In case Randy and I aren't able to set aside enough for our child's college or our retirement, today I sold some of the stock that Mom invested for me, then bought 10,000 shares of Apple Computers at $2.84 per share.

I know, I know. I'm cashing in on my knowledge of the future. This is my compensation for going through puberty and menopause twice. I promise to be completely detached from the fortune I make when I sell the stock at its all-time high, just before Apple is bought out by Samsung.

You would do the same. Right?

Ron Frazer

Dr. Ron Frazer has degrees in mechanical engineering, mathematics, natural health and ninety percent of a degree in fine arts that he'll probably never finish. Apparently he doesn't know what he wants to be when he grows up.

He has lived in the US, the UK, St. Lucia and Grenada. He currently lives in a suburb of Cleveland, Ohio. On the odd occasions when he chooses reality, he lives with his naturopath wife Sandy, and a domineering Chihuahua.

Ron also plays a bad clarinet; a version of bad that makes his dog howl.

Novels

Beyond a Veil explores the spiritual growth of a woman who is dealing with her daughter's murder while struggling with a terminal illness. While it sounds like a sob story, her spiritual growth is quite exemplary and the tone is very light-hearted.

Time Branches, the story of a woman in a coma who discovers she can move in time and space. Through a series of jumps, she takes herself further and further back in her own life as she attempts to improve the outcomes of the lives of her mother and sister. She has a bit of naughty fun in the process.

The Carib's Smile, the first book of the *Jacinta Joseph Caribbean Adventure trilogy*, follows the adventures of a black female detective who returns to the Caribbean island where she was born, then becomes dedicated to cleaning up the corruption that is holding the country back while murdering anyone that stands in its way. The trilogy is written as both a mystery and a romantic comedy.

The Judge's wife, the second novel of the *Jacinta Joseph Caribbean Adventure trilogy*, finds the detective joining eight other grandmothers who are intent on changing the government while she is immersed in an ocean of family problems.

The Wife's Turn is the final Jacinta Joseph Caribbean adventure where the remaining bad guys are dealt with and the economy revamped.

A Handful of Seawater, Ron's first novel, is a fictional biography of Morgan, a junk-yard dog of a boy, who starts life as the poorest of the poor on a tropical island. Read the touching story of an orphan's triumph under the Zen-like guidance of a simple fisherman who mentors him. It's a story of sex, drugs and Reggae but from the perspective of a young man's search for love, family and fulfillment.

Short Fiction

Ron's poems and short stories have been published in *Sandscript, The Blackwater Review, and The African-American Review*. His stories are based on the lives of his students and their families on the Caribbean island of Grenada where he taught math and science following the 1983 US intervention.

Non-Fiction

Staying Well: a family guide to wellness is a compilation of articles that were written as the Natural Health guru for a website. Ron has a Masters and a Ph.D. in Natural Health from Clayton College in Birmingham, AL.

Websites

Books: www.ronfrazer.com

Facebook: facebook.com/RonFrazerAuthor

Blog: ronfrazer.com/blog

Art Credits

Cover art by Gerd Altman, pixabay.com

Cover and book design by Ron Frazer

www.ingramcontent.com/pod-product-compliance
Lightning Source LLC
Chambersburg PA
CBHW030643110726
47901CB00002B/547